"Want To Join Me In A Housewarming?"

Roberta had to smile. "We might do that another time. I'm busy tonight. But we ought not to get in the habit of sharing a meal. Because I'm a lobbyist, I go to a lot of parties, so I'm rarely here for the evening meal."

Graham nodded. "I wasn't trying to tie you down to a schedule."

"Thank you."

"Here's my list of numbers where you can reach me if you ever need me for anything."

None of her female apartmentmates had ever done anything like that. Roberta was touched by his gesture, and it made her a little cautious. She took the list hesitantly and again said, "Thank you." Maybe sharing an apartment with a man wasn't going to be as simple as she'd thought. She would have to be formal and a little aloof. Cool.

She said, "Welcome. I hope we get along well and don't interfere with each other at all."

Standing there in the living room in his sweaty jogging suit, he watched her walk away from him and out of sight beyond that mysterious door, which was always closed. She had just told him to keep his distance. Clearly, that was what she had done. Now how was he going to handle that?

Dear Reader:

Six down, six to go... It's July, and I hope you've been enjoying our "Year of the Man." From January to December, 1989 is a twelve-month extravaganza at Silhouette Desire. We're spotlighting one book each month with special cover treatment as a tribute to the Silhouette Desire hero—our *Man of the Month*!

Created by your favorite authors, these men are utterly irresistible. One of Lass Small's Lambert sisters gets a very special man in July. *Man of the Month* Graham Rawlins may start as the *Odd Man Out*, but that doesn't last long....

And Mr. August, Joyce Thies's *Mountain Man* thinks he's conquered it all by facing Alaska, America's last frontier—but he hasn't met his mail-order bride yet!

Yours,

Isabel Swift
Senior Editor & Editorial Coordinator

LASS SMALL
Odd Man Out

Silhouette Desire

Published by Silhouette Books New York

America's Publisher of Contemporary Romance

SILHOUETTE BOOKS
300 East 42nd St., New York, N.Y. 10017

ISBN: 0-373-05505-6

First Silhouette Books printing July 1989

Printed in the U.S.A.

Books by Lass Small

Silhouette Romance

An Irritating Man #444
Snow Bird #521

Silhouette Desire

Tangled Web #241
To Meet Again #322
Stolen Day #341
Possibles #356
Intrusive Man #373
To Love Again #397
Blindman's Bluff #413
Goldilocks and the Behr #437
Hide and Seek #453
Red Rover #491
Odd Man Out #505

LASS SMALL

finds that living on this planet at this time is a fascinating experience. People are amazing. She thinks that to be a teller of tales of people, places and things is absolutely marvelous.

Of all the Lambert sisters, Roberta was the one who wasn't clear to me. So I began by seeing her from Graham's point of view, and it became his story. None of us knows another person completely, but you will know Graham and, through him, you will begin to understand Roberta.

One

It was just after the New Year when Graham Rawlins greeted his friend with a grin. "So how's D.C.'s most chased Don Juan?" Graham had a lazy Midwest accent.

Approaching Graham's desk, there in the Department of Justice building, Jim looked a little tired. Instead of a flippant reply, he frowned.

With humorous exasperation, Graham protested, "Look at all the clever answers you could have given, with that opening. Like 'tired' or 'holding up' or— Have you ever considered what you owe me as a straight man? I feed you the best lines you get."

Graham noted that Jim wasn't paying any attention. He hesitated, as if trying to decide how to begin. The two men were lawyers. In that town comprised mostly of politicians, lobbyists and the ramifications of government, the fact that someone spoke with care wasn't unusual. Jim chose words just as carefully as anybody else, but he never gave the appearance of speaking cautiously. Now he clearly sorted words.

Curiously watching his friend, Graham told him, "If you were my boss, by now I'd be convinced you were getting up the nerve to fire me. For mercy's sake, don't forget to thank me for my hard work all these four years, and be sure to tell me I've made a valuable contribution to our government." He'd just completed a week-long management seminar.

Jim smiled a little because he thought he should. He usually spoke with a clipped, Eastern accent, but now his words were oddly spaced. "It's a similar undertaking to a firing, in that I would lose you as a companion."

Graham began to pay attention. Since Jim continued to give him a probing look, Graham smiled a little. "Now I am curious. What's up? I'm being sent to Timbuktu?"

Jim glanced around the office, which had quickly emptied at six o'clock. He took a slow, deep breath before he said, "There aren't too many men I'd give this to, so I want you to be impressed." His hard, level look came back to Graham as he continued, "There's a woman I've met who has had enough of female apartmentmates. She's decided to interview men to share her place out in Alexandria—now wait! Don't even begin to think what you're thinking. This is strictly business."

Graham's lips had parted in surprise, but now he frowned a little and asked, "Why not you? I know you've been looking for a place closer in."

Jim appeared to choose his words more carefully. "I'm not looking for a wife. Bob is a..." He hesitated to describe her.

"Who's this Bob?"

"It's the woman I've been talking about." His hands in his pockets, Jim turned to pace a step or two, as a lawyer would in giving information to a jury. "Her name is Roberta Lambert. She's from Texas. She's... special."

Under such circumstances, it was natural that Graham should ask, "If this Bob is so special, why are you giving her to me like this?"

In excellent courtroom candor, Jim replied logically: "It's time you considered getting married—"

Graham let go a disbelieving laugh that sputtered through deliberately tightened lips.

"I'm serious. You've been running around loose long enough. You have to look around while there are still choices among the women you meet, before they're all married or divorced and cluttered up with somebody else's kids or something like that."

And again, being a lawyer, Graham inquired, "Why is it time I got married and not you? You're thirty-two, a year older than I, and if it's time I was married, then it's past time for you."

Jim nodded seriously, looking at his shoes. "I know. I plan to."

"Really?" Graham was surprised. "Who's the gem?"

Jim shook his head slowly and pushed up his lower lip.

It finally hit Graham that Jim was having a hard time with this exchange. Why would Jim make a gift of a woman he thought Graham should seriously consider? Suspiciously Graham inquired, "Is this Bob an old lover of yours that you can't shake off?"

Jim's stare was so hostile that Graham's head moved back an inch to indicate he recognized Jim's objection to the words.

Then it was Graham's turn to frown. "I don't get this at all. You say you know her. You obviously are ready to defend her. But you're not interested in moving in with her and taking your chances, even though you admit you want to marry, but not her, and you're willing that I try for her. What *is* all this?"

Still hostile, Jim didn't want to say anything more, but he felt compelled to explain. "You have to know how important my career is to me. I can't be distracted from it. I'm at the point where I have clout. But I want power. I need a particular kind of woman. Bob isn't she."

"So. What's the matter with her?"

"Nothing!" Jim's breathing had picked up, along with his irritation.

"Is she pregnant?"

Jim's eyes flared and he stood up straight, his feet planted in a belligerent way. "You're treading on eggs. She is not."

Graham, too, straightened. He, too, was very serious. "I think I need some more from you on this. Why are you nudging me in the way of a woman you don't want? What's the matter with her?"

"Up until this minute, you and I have been good friends. I'm closer to you than I am to most people. I respect you. I believe you're a good man. Bob isn't for me." He slid his hands back into his pockets as he continued. "She thinks she doesn't want to get married. She's a lawyer, she works as an environmental lobbyist, and she's very dedicated. She thinks she's a career woman. She isn't. She's a nest builder. She needs to get married to a man who will treat her right and give her some nice kids and love her enough to let her think it's all her idea. You."

Softly, again Graham asked, "Why not you?"

"Because I could love her!" he replied simply. "My career comes first. I need to get her safely married so that I can give up thinking about her and being tempted."

Graham wasn't surprised, oddly enough. "Have you slept with her?"

Impatient and frowning, Jim said an abrupt "No! I don't know her very well. I've only seen her a couple of times. She's different."

Graham responded softly, "Well, I'll be damned."

"She's looking for a male apartmentmate. If you have any sense, you won't waste any time getting over there and applying. Don't give her any indication that you see her as a woman. Pretend you're only looking for enough space and easy commute to work. Be businesslike and drive a good bargain. Offer to carry out the garbage and help with the cleaning for less than half the rent." He turned back sternly to add, "Be sure you give your full half, but make her bargain with you. That will make her think you're not interested in her."

A little exasperated, Graham asked the ceiling. "How can I marry a girl named Bob?"

"If you play your cards right and you're damned lucky, you might find out. Just be braced so that when you see her you don't make a complete jackass of yourself and lie down on the floor with all your legs up in the air in surrender."

"I must admit you have made me a tad curious."

"If you give her any grief, you answer to me."

"You're not foolish. You're not the type to set me up as a joke. Can I believe all this?"

Jim's reply was, "Believe it."

So Graham decided he'd be clever and do poor old stupid Jim a favor and help Cupid get this couple together. He called for an appointment.

Roberta Lambert had a pleasant, rather throaty voice and was strictly business. She requested references, credit rating and the names of four friends.

With Jim's cautioning to be firm and bargain, Graham requested identical information about the snooty Miss Lambert.

She was unruffled, and complied. Apparently she had expected him to ask, as a logical request, and he gained a point in his favor by doing exactly that.

He didn't list Jim as one of his friends. Somehow it seemed wiser that if this Cupid business was to work, he should make it all seem by chance. Happenstance. The best happenstances are those that are contrived. He smiled. It always lifted his spirits to give a friend something, or arrange a pleasure for someone else— especially on a rotten January day that made even D.C. look as if it was just another big, ugly city.

While Graham waited for Bob, this Roberta Lambert from Texas, to contact his friends and references and check his bank, he passed her office, going out of his way by only three buildings. He looked around the beehive of the environmental agency as he tried to sort out which woman was the one who had the power to tempt Jim McFarland into giving up his ambitions.

After a pleasurable examination of the busy women, Graham chose five "possibles." Why hadn't he gotten a description of Roberta? Hair color would have helped. At this point he couldn't ask any of her references to describe her. He wouldn't want them to tell her that he'd asked. He wasn't supposed to be interested in her. Not as a woman.

It was two days later when Jim called to ask, "Have you seen her?"

Graham smiled. The besotted man hadn't even said who. So Graham asked, "Who?"

"You know damned good and well who. Quit being cute."

Graham laughed heartlessly and replied, "Not yet. What's she look like?"

There was a pause and a deeply indrawn breath before Jim said plainly, "Brunette, long hair, blue eyes."

"Well, that eliminates half of the women in D.C. Tall? Short? Fat? Th—"

"Medium height and build . . . beautiful."

"Good. We're down to about one hundred thousand—"

But Jim had hung up.

That made Graham thoughtful. While he had considered this something of a lark, it was serious for Jim.

Therefore, when the call came for an interview and an inspection of the apartment, Graham wasn't quite so open to her. He drove to Alexandria, critically noting bus stops and looking around the area. There was a small shopping center, and the apartment buildings were big, rectangular rabbit warrens. So were those in Roberta's complex, but they'd been set askew so that the trees hadn't all been cut away.

Graham got out and looked around at the varieties of tall trees: pine, maple and oak. He acknowledged the dollop of imagination that had caused the identical buildings to be put up as separate structures so that there was the feeling of difference. He wanted to live there.

If the Lambert vixen was halfway tolerable, he'd take the deal. Then he walked around the building to find her door number. It was away from the parking area, on the ground floor. And it was then he saw the stream.

It ran busily through the uneven, sloping terrain, and it was perfect. The water was clear, revealing rocks and sand in its wandering bed. There were a couple of natural slate waterfalls that fell a foot or two. There were gray squirrels running around. It always surprised him to see squirrels that were gray. Back home, in Indiana, the squirrels were an orangy brown. He smiled at the creatures, the trees, the stream and the peace. It was just right. Even if he had to bend a little to suit the woman, he'd take this deal; or if she was impossible, he'd find another apartment in this complex.

So his face was serious as he rang her doorbell, but he still wasn't really prepared for her. Even knowing that she'd zonked Jim McFarland, Graham wasn't braced enough.

She opened the door and looked at him. The top of her head would be just past his shoulder, her face was scrubbed, her long, dark hair was pulled back into a ponytail, and she looked sixteen. He almost asked if her mother was there. He knew Roberta Lambert was twenty-nine.

With an easy courteousness that was automatic, inbred, she said, "You're Graham Rawlins. How do you do? I'm Roberta Lambert." He was taller than she thought he'd be, and he was a little overwhelming. He'd make the apartment seem small. Thank goodness he was blond. She'd never much cared for blonds.

He stared, but he managed to nod once, as if he was weighing her dubious "plus" qualities against a great number of minuses. The grave balancing of pluses and minuses was taught for a whole semester in law school. It was like doctors being grilled for a year about acting like gods. It didn't take as much time to learn to be dubious as it did to play a god.

But she, too, was a lawyer. You can't fool a fooler, she thought, and she gave him a patient look. He said a belated "I'm doing well, and you?"

"Fine. Come in and look around." She had stepped back to allow him to come inside.

It was then he noted that she wore a cast on her right hand. He was appalled that she had been hurt. This flower. He saw that she waited for him to react to something, and glanced around. She was showing him the living room.

It was atypical of rentals. In the rectangular area, the furniture and rug were the safe, bland type. She'd added a charming old padded walnut chair with an ornately carved back. And on the sofa was a richly colored plush throw of oranges and browns, that lifted the whole room. There weren't any plastic flowers.

She walked over and opened a door that was a little more than halfway down the right side of the living room. "This is the room and bath over here. On the other side—" she gestured to the left "—is the dining room with a kitchen, and beyond that is my room and bath. It's a good arrangement to share."

He added, "Unless you give wild parties and don't invite me. And I'm trapped next to the living room, trying to hear the jokes through the wall." He finally stopped his tongue and gave her an inquiring look, as if he wasn't really babbling along but was rather cleverly questioning her about wild parties.

She replied, "I rarely give parties, none of which would be wild." She stood, waiting for him to inspect his area.

He noted she hadn't said anything about inviting him to her un-wild parties. He entered the doorway into a small hall. Ahead of him was an empty, shallow linen closet. To his right was the door to the bedroom. He went inside and inspected the utilitarian room, which held a plain double bed, a chest of drawers and a kneehole desk with a lamp and phone. The closet space wasn't bad.

She waited in his little hall as he looked into the rather small bathroom. He turned on the water in the tub and watched how it drained. Then he flushed the toilet. Everything seemed to work, and he was enormously pleased he'd tried it all, because it made him appear dubious.

She led him back across the living room into the kitchen-dining area. He did realize that she expected some reaction from him and he couldn't just say "Fine." He stood and looked around in what he hoped was a judgmental way. He tried the garbage-disposal unit, looked at the empty cupboard that would be his, inspected his part of the freezer and the shelves allotted to him in the refrigerator. He did this with his eyebrows slightly raised and his lower lip protruding just a bit. He felt as if he should have on white gloves and run a finger along the ridges and surfaces. He smiled. He couldn't be too asinine, only justly judicious.

She didn't show him her room. He bet it was frilly and smelled deliciously female. He wanted to see it. She stood in the way. He questioned, "Your room?"

She gave him a look as if any fool would have figured that out already, but she was gracious enough to nod once, agreeing it was, indeed, her room.

He studied her briefly. This was a woman Jim had firmly avoided. Graham frowned over the thought and looked at the dining-room table, on which lay a scattering of papers.

She invited, "Shall we sit here?"

And he understood her maneuver. It was more businesslike than the living room. And she'd seen to it that only two of the four chairs were at the table so they sat across from one another, like adversaries.

She shifted the papers. "Everything split right down the middle. Rent, utilities, fees."

"What sort of fees?"

"Grounds care. Maintenance."

This was where he was supposed to bargain and appear indifferent. "What if I agree to do the dirty work, in return for less than half the rent?"

"If you can't afford even half the rent, you have no business looking for an apartment in this area. I would require a full month's rent in advance to ensure your not running out and leaving me in the lurch." She gave him a plain look.

He smiled a little. "No adjustments if I promise to carry out the garbage?"

Coolly, she informed him, "With a disposal, there is very little garbage. It's no problem."

"Well, I think this will be just fine."

"If you have any reservations, you have the weekend to think it over. I have two other people who want interviews." That wasn't true. They'd called, but she hadn't been able to pin them down as to who they were, exactly. This Graham Rawlins was the only one who'd checked out fully and well. And his bank said he could indeed afford the rent.

Graham leaned back and looked around the kitchen, the part of the living room that he could see, and at her closed door. "I think this is very nice. I like that little stream. I believe I'd have accepted a squatter's cabin if that stream went along with it." He watched as she smiled for the first time, and he quickly sucked in air—he was so thrilled by her. Then he became still, as if she would bolt if he moved.

She studied his regular features, his blond hair with contrasting dark eyebrows and lashes. She told him, "You're very good-looking."

At the last possible minute, he managed to stop a pleased smile that she thought so. He waited soberly.

"I refuse to answer your phone for you. And I won't tolerate overnights with cosy breakfasts in the morning. It's against my morals, and it's inconvenient. I've put up with this sort of thing with a couple of the women who've shared this place, and the men felt chatty and have had no hesitancy about eating from my food supply. And they don't wash dishes. I find it very irritating. It's best we understand this now."

He clarified: "And the same for you. No overnights."

"Why, of course not. And we'll be sure to clean up after ourselves. No stacked dishes."

He added: "As long as the rules go both ways."

"Naturally. Family overnights are okay."

He nodded. "I can agree to that."

"But no 'kissing cousins' who go around half-dressed."

He smiled. "Deal."

"And you may not give my phone number to any of your women."

"Why would I do that?"

"The women have, so if their line is busy, their men would call me or leave messages on my tape. I don't care for that at all."

"Both ways. And I, too, have an answering machine. Anything else?"

"No food poaching. Not without permission or invitation."

"That's not unreasonable."

"Let me know by Monday."

"I'm ready now. The stream sold me." That's what he said, all right; he'd heard the words go right out of his adroit mouth. He didn't throw himself down on his knees and plead or anything. He just talked about the stream. He wrote checks, and he got a new key since the locks had been changed, and he said goodbye. He'd been so brilliant that he hadn't even asked how she'd broken her hand. Nor had he offered to kiss it well.

He moved two days later on Friday, forfeiting the rest of the month's rent on his fifth-floor, two-window apartment. He thought coming in so soon might seem a little pushy, but Roberta wasn't anywhere around. He had to rent a storage closet in the maintenance building to hold some of his things: skis, golf cart and summer clothing. But he settled into the quiet place. He thought his oversize TV screen helped the blah living room considerably, but he put his electronic keyboard in his room.

He grocery-shopped, came back, filled his cupboards and his share of the freezer and refrigerator. And he was there—with a blue-eyed, dark-haired witch who lured men off their chosen paths. Well, she'd tempted James McFarland.

And, oh, yes. *He* was going to play Cupid and get them together and make Jim grateful to Graham Rawlins all the rest of his life. Well. He hadn't told Jim he was going to do that. It wasn't as if he'd committed himself, it could be that she really wasn't suitable for good old Jim.

Graham thought it just might be best if he waited a while before he ruined Jim's life altogether by forcing him into something he was trying to avoid. It didn't pay to go against good sense. Jim was a levelheaded man and full-grown. Nobody had to run his life for him, and if he decided he didn't want a woman, why force it?

The next day, Graham was awakened by a friend's call, but Graham declined the offered outing. He wanted to see Roberta. He hung up the phone, pulled on jeans and went out into the kitchen. She wasn't there and hadn't left a note.

At noon, Graham made pasta for two, but she didn't show up, and he ate it alone. After washing the few dishes meticulously, he put them away neatly. Then he went out and walked along the charming, shallow stream, which wandered busily over sand and rocks among the six blocks of apartment buildings. It was an adult complex—those in residence were young, upwardly mobile professionals, junior executives and strivers. There was no time for children, so there were very few competing with Graham for sole ownership of the stream.

He went back to her apartment—his apartment—and looked around more closely. There were books about whales and nuclear waste and all of Rachel Carson's books. The framed pictures were of wide mountains, buffalo on an endless yellow prairie, and Indians sitting on horses and looking far away. Ah, yes; environmental lobbyist.

In her living room, along one side of a chair, there was a wooden basket with richly blue wool skeins and something that was being knitted. Jim had said she was a nest builder. Other than the old chair, the plush throw and the knitting, he really didn't see much evidence of nesting. No doilies. No cake waiting on the counter. He wondered how she'd broken her hand. Slipped and fallen? Wrestling a recalcitrant lemming that didn't want to be saved from the sea?

Graham restlessly roamed around and finally knocked on her bedroom door, but there was no answer. There was no sound at all. He knew she wasn't there.

He made a treat—Rice Krispies mixed with a jar of melted marshmallows—and set it out on the counter. He might just as well be living alone. He played his keyboard for a long time, using the headphones and being filled with the music. Then he went out and walked along the stream again. From watching some joggers, he located a track that circled the outer edge of the compound. It made a very nice run, there among the trees. One circle was six blocks.

He returned to the apartment and changed into jogging clothes and shoes, then went back and ran three miles. When he returned to the apartment he was all sweaty and smelly, and she was there. He didn't know quite how to act. So he asked, "Everything okay?"

Roberta thought he looked incredibly masculine. He seemed to fill the room, just as she'd thought he would. There was no room left for her. Her own space. He was crowding her. He and that *humongous* TV. "I don't believe I've ever seen a screen quite that large."

He grinned proudly. "It's new. With football, it's just like you're right in there with them. It's great."

Football appalled her. Along with her concern for whales, she worried about football players. "Do you play?"

"Not anymore." He moved a little to show off his body as he went on. "I'm out of shape. Office." He gestured to indicate his life's limitations. She looked down his body, and his entire skin surface knew it. He breathed through his mouth and blurted, "How did you hurt your hand?"

She lifted it and frowned at it in annoyance. "A purse snatcher. I broke his nose. The cast has been a real nuisance."

Her protectiveness didn't cover purse snatchers. If she broke her hand when she broke the guy's nose, she must have splattered him! Graham looked at her with some respect. "I think you could learn to enjoy football. The Super Bowl is just four weeks from tomorrow."

She replied dismissively, "Although Texas is football crazy, that particular blight never touched our family. I have four sisters."

"Your dad never had a chance," he said in sympathy.

"His particular variety of mayhem is rodeo bronco-busting. He terrifies us all. It's like race-car driving. Men like to risk their necks."

"Rodeo?"

"They band a horse's— They tie the horse uncomfortably, and he gets mad. The men try to ride him for a set number of *seconds*. Just that fact tells you how stupid it is."

"I see. I just like football. I don't ride a horse, and I drive carefully."

She was a little disgruntled as she looked at that enormous screen. She hadn't taken football into consideration when she opted for a male to share her apartment—although she'd heard tales of wives who wailed and pulled their hair all through football season. Now there were even videotapes. A man could replay any game, any time—*all year*. He could watch a discussion of any position—by coaches and people who played that position, and those whose job it was to thwart that position—with examples of smashing bodies and impossible catches of both footballs and bodies. Roberta became a little depressed.

"I made some Rice Krispie treat. May I cut some off for you? How about some cocoa? It's another couple of hours until supper, and I thought I'd grill a steak. Want to join me in a housewarming? I've just moved in."

She had to smile back. "We might do that another time. I'm busy tonight. But we ought not to get in the habit of sharing a meal. Then one has to wait for the other, and the food budgets get tangled up."

"Well, I did want to talk about that. I find I leave a half hour earlier than you in the mornings. So I'm up before you. I might just as well make enough coffee for us both. Okay? And I'll be home a half hour or more before you in the evenings. I might just as well put in a potato or thaw something like that. I wouldn't mind."

"Because I'm a lobbyist, I go to a lot of parties, so I'm rarely here for the evening meal. Legislators will be coming back the middle of the month for the State of the Union address, and the fund-raisers will be non-stop from then on."

"What sort of fund-raisers?"

"They are almost always exclusively given by various members of House and Senate. They're scheduled after working hours and on weekdays. And they are expensive. The least amount is about two hundred dollars a ticket. That's for the little gatherings. There are also elaborate dinners that cost the guests much more. I go to these affairs because it's a way to speak personally to the people who will vote on legislation that affects the environment. I have to remind them how concerned we are, and about what. It's part of my job."

Graham nodded. "I wasn't trying to tie you down to a schedule. I just meant that if you leave me a note at night about what you need done, I'd be glad to do it. Sometimes you eat better if it doesn't take so long to fix something."

"Thank you."

"Here's my list of numbers where you can reach me if you ever need me for anything."

No apartment-sharing female had ever done anything like that. Roberta was touched by his gesture, and it made her a little cautious. She took the list hesitantly and again said, "Thank you." Maybe having a man as an apartmentmate wasn't going to be as simple as she'd thought. She would have to be formal and a little aloof. Cool.

She declined the Rice Krispies-marshmallow treat. "I'm watching my weight. I have to go to too many things where there is plenty to nibble. But thank you. I believe I'll lie down for a while.'' She looked back at him and said belatedly, "Welcome. I hope we get along well and don't interfere with each other at all."

Standing there in the living room in his sweaty jogging suit, he watched her walk away from him and out of sight beyond that mysterious door, which was always closed. She had just told him to keep his distance. Clearly, *that* was what she had done. Now, how was he going to handle that?

She came out of that room about seven that evening and it was just fortunate he was sitting down. She had her hair up in a swirl and wore long, dangly earrings. Her blue dress sparkled here and there, as she breathed. She even had a covering of the same material around her cast. She was smashing.

He said, "You clean up pretty good."

She nodded to acknowledge that, then she smiled a bit.

With applaudable casualness he inquired, "Date?"

"No. A big dinner with a group of old friends." She smiled up at him. "Good night."

And he was left alone.

Two

It was about an hour after Roberta left that the cable people came and hooked up Graham's TV, and he got all the movie channels. His mother would have had a fit.

When he was growing up, his mother would say, "Now, Graham, you can read a good book in the time it would take to watch a movie." She'd never really taken to films. Not even *Gone with the Wind*. Every other person's mother in all the country had seen that movie at least once, but not his mother.

Graham looked over the choices and laid out the night's viewing. It was Saturday night and he hadn't really expected to spend it this way.

After his first glance at Roberta, his unrealistic subconscious had assumed she would be there that night. They'd have a nice charcoaled steak, a salad and the champagne he'd bought for his...housewarming. That idea hadn't been at all farfetched—not until she'd come out of her room at seven o'clock, all duded up and ready to leave.

He let his eyes be occupied with the screen while his mind figured out Roberta. Actually, what he was figuring was his mind's *view* of Roberta. What man could figure out a woman? The way he saw it, it was all Jim's fault. He'd said that Bob was a nest builder. That caused a specific mental image of a sweet and helpful woman, domesticated and cooperative. The premise had been misleading. She didn't even eat at home. She went out. How domesticated was that?

There was always the chance this was some sort of revenge perpetrated by Jim for some slight Graham couldn't remember. Had he ever taken a woman away from Jim? Outside of it being hilariously ridiculous for him even to have tried, Graham knew full well that he had not.

Had a case been assigned to him that Jim had coveted? Quite the contrary, he'd been given cases by Jim, who had encouraged Graham. Jim had been something of a mentor. And Graham had always given Jim full credit.

Graham went into the kitchen and removed the bottle of champagne from his part of the refrigerator; wiggled the cork to loosen it in the professional, two-thumb, non-pop way; and went back to sit down in the living room with a water glass full. He drank a toast to the apartment, to his new big-screen TV and to his absent roomie.

He had champagne with Rice Krispies-marshmallow treat. And he watched a steamy film where the man didn't appreciate what he had and the woman suffered. He turned over to the sports channel and watched two segments on the NFL—one on tight ends and the other on noseguards. Then the station treated viewers to a portion of the crunch tape. If Roberta saw that, she'd probably faint.

The late show was just beginning when Roberta came home. The screen was still showing trailers for other films. He rose politely and helped her get her cast free of her coat sleeve as he said, "You're just in time to watch *The Big Easy* again."

"It's on? I never got to see it."

"Be my guest," he said magnanimously, bowing a little. "And you may have some of my housewarming champagne."

Roberta's lips parted just a little as she realized that he had spent Saturday night alone, and he'd planned a slight celebration of his first weekend of sharing her apartment. He meant to be friendly. The film would be a treat, and she intended to be cordial with her tenant. She could sleep late tomorrow. "Don't let it start without me!" she yelled and ran for her door.

He followed to the edge of the living room, and from across the dining area he got to see inside her door—to a linen closet just like his. Her secret life was still safe from him.

He hurried to get another glass as he swallowed a little smile, and back in the living room, he sat not quite in the middle of the sofa. A great feeling of peace settled over him. It was as if he'd striven all night toward a hopeless goal, and he'd finally reached it. He was going to become friendly with Jim's elusive and delicious-looking temptress.

Graham awaited her return, yelling "Hurry!" with delight. He felt a little animated and sternly controlled himself. He yelled again, "Hurry!" He made his voice deeper and more masculine.

"I'm coming. I'm coming!" she called, and pretty soon she rushed in and stood watching the screen as the film began. "My word," she said, awed. "It's just like a theater, the screen's so huge."

"Yeah." He smiled, so pleased. "Sit down."

She perched on the edge of the couch, still amazed with the screen, and was immediately involved in the story.

He'd seen it three times and just let his eyes watch her. She'd changed into a blue lounge suit that was soft and marvelous on her body. Maybe the lounge suit wasn't marvelous; maybe it was just her body. She didn't wear a bra. He had to breathe through his mouth in order not to sound like an excited bull. Eventually he noticed that she'd smeared cream on her face, one-handedly, and was wiping it off with tissues. Gradually she was becoming sixteen again. She wore fuzzy slippers on her feet.

She accepted comments from him, but mostly she was absorbed with the movie. She laughed nicely when the hero sassily reached over and dipped his fingers into the startled heroine's décolletage to see if she was wearing a hidden microphone.

Graham put a glass of champagne into Roberta's good hand, and she sipped it. He smiled and settled back, watching her but keeping track of the story in case she discussed something.

At one point she stood up and moved sideways to the opening into the kitchen, her eyes never leaving the screen. Then she ducked out of sight and came back with a very large bag of popped popcorn. She shared, and after her lecture about keeping hands off each other's food supply, the sharing of the popcorn touched him. She was really generous.

Generous? He was giving her champagne, and he thought she was generous because she shared popcorn? Come on, Graham, let's not go overboard here. Well, it was a start in the right direction. Who knew what she might share under the right circumstances? He smiled at her profile... all the way down.

He was curious as to how she'd take the steamy bedroom scene, and he gave up seeing it in order to watch her. She didn't look aside or appear to be embarrassed about it. Then he saw her lick her lips, and he was more affected by her than by anything on the screen.

Could such a delicious-looking woman be sensual? My God, he thought, what if she was everything a man could want? And Jim McFarland had glimpsed it in her and wanted it all. Did she feel the same way about Jim? What if she was as affected by Jim as he was about her? Graham needed to know.

Troubled, impatient, restless, he waited endlessly for the film to end. And in the waiting, he realized he would really be troubled if she cared for Jim. Jim wasn't for her. He was too involved with his place in the world. He wanted to be a wheeler-dealer who had power. He wanted to be part of the summit meetings. He wanted to make a difference in the world. What would happen to a fragile, precious woman like Roberta if she was ignored by such a man?

On the sofa beside Graham, that fragile, precious woman was taking down her hair, and it fell in a heavy swirl around her shoulders. She looked like a wood nymph, a Lady of the Lake, something magical. Graham began to feel sorry for Jim. And a mental replay of their initial conversation made Graham know how hard it had been for Jim to turn this woman over to another man—to him. Jim had given her to him.

Now all Graham had to do was find out if she wanted Jim. Or if there was some other man she loved. Surely not. Graham tried to marshal all his good deeds to bargain with God to be on his side. Graham racked his brain and couldn't turn up anything worth calling to God's attention. He began to despair.

Graham found that the endless time did pass and the film was over. He asked, "Do you—"

But Roberta was saying, "This was so nice. I've never had cable. And I rarely get to a theater. Thank you for such a nice treat."

"There's a cable extension that's easy to hook up, if you have a television in your room. I didn't go in to look."

"Thank you for that. I don't believe I'll have the hookup. I'd be up all night, watching."

He tried a second time. "Do you—"

"The champagne was better than what we had tonight. Here's to a pleasant association." She lifted her glass of long-dead bubbles.

He could drink to that, but he mentally replaced "association" with "relationship." He asked, "Do you—" since she didn't interrupt that time, he could continue "—know Jim McFarland?" He held his breath.

She'd been folding down the top of the popcorn sack with one hand and hadn't really heard, so she asked, "Jimmie Carlin?"

Something exciting flickered through him. But he couldn't leave it. He corrected, "Jim McFarland."

"No. Is he connected with the EPA?"

"He's a lawyer with the feds."

"I don't believe I know him. Is he a friend of yours? Why do you ask? Is he someone I should know?"

"No, no. I just wondered." She *didn't* remember Jim.

"I meet so many people while lobbying that I never remember them all. I wish I could. I concentrate on those faces and names that can help us."

"So it's not just a job."

"No."

He was impressed that she didn't feel the need then to campaign in order to win him to her interest in the environment. She said it simply and left it that way. Then he stood when she did, and he watched her stretch her arms up without any self-consciousness. He had to clench his hands to keep from reaching out to her. And he'd been with her only twice now. That was how many times Jim had said he'd seen her. Think of that. Jim had only seen her a couple of times, and he had *known*.

"This has been very nice. Welcome to apartment 108. May our association be as pleasant as it's been this evening."

"Yes."

They shook left hands since she wore the cast on her right hand, and he wondered if that was bad luck. Somewhere along his life, he seemed to remember that shaking left hands was bad luck. It made him look at her soberly.

"Good night," she said.

He echoed her words and watched her walk through the dining area and disappear through the magic door. Then he went back to sit on the sofa and look over to the cushion where she'd sat. He put his hand over it and curled the fingers as if to capture the essence of her, so recently there. It felt cool to his heat.

Deep in disturbed thoughts, he turned off the screen and sat quietly in the dark silence. One good thing: she didn't remember Jim. But then, maybe it was just Jim's name she didn't remember. Maybe she lay in that mysterious room and dreamed of Jim. How was Graham going to find out?

He'd have to arrange a confrontation. How could he? If she didn't remember Jim, why tempt fate by calling her attention to him? Jim was a formidable man. He wasn't D.C.'s Don Juan for nothing. Graham Rawlins had never come even close to being anything to compare with Jim.

But Graham had to know if she could be tempted by another man—by Jim. If Jim could be so attracted that he would try to eliminate the attraction, then the woman he looked upon in that way would have known it. No human female could be that unknowing if Jim was interested in her. But Roberta didn't recall his name.

Graham knew he was getting entirely away from his role as Cupid. Now he didn't even want them to see each other. All's fair in love and war. Was this love? How could it possibly be love? He'd seen her twice. But he felt a readiness for it to be love. Why was that? Was Jim right when he claimed Graham was ready to settle down? Spring was going to be coming along in a couple of months, and his sap was rising just a little early.

Reluctantly Graham faced the fact that, before anything went any further, Jim should have one final chance to claim Roberta. Graham admitted that. He'd do it out of honor. Hell, he thought gloomily. His mother had been a damned stickler for honorable conduct. If she knew her lectures had borne fruit, she'd be so amazed. If he survived this testing, he might tell her. She ought to feel she'd made an impression.

And if he lost? If he lost, he'd give his mother a tape of *Gone with the Wind* and a VCR next Christmas. It would be a subtle revenge. He'd be able to afford it, because if Jim and Roberta saw each other again, Graham Rawlins would be odd man out.

On Sunday, Roberta came home from church after the football game had started, and the fact that Graham hadn't gone to church in some long time gave him a flicker of guilt. He could have used some "plus" points about now. As she came inside, she smiled at him, and Graham rose and reached to help her with her coat, but Roberta waved him away. She managed to remove it in spite of her cast.

She was drawn to that big screen. He realized it, and he wasn't so embroiled in the action that he didn't know when she'd left the room. He was aware she'd gone, and was nigglingly distracted from the play by her absence.

But she returned, in that insidiously soft, blue lounge suit of velvet, and wearing the incongruous fuzzy slippers. She was again creaming off her makeup. Perched on the edge of the sofa, she watched the game with something like fascinated horror. She bit a knuckle when a man limped off the field supported by others. And she straightened anxiously when one lay writhing in pain.

"He's okay. He just got hit wrong."

She looked at Graham indignantly. "There's a right way to get hit?"

"Well, there are more comfortable ways."

During halftime the two watchers scrambled to the kitchen and got something together for a late lunch. They were again settled on the sofa for the second half.

She did know the rudiments of football. "Games and the rules were part of required physical training in gym classes at any school." So she did know the object was to get the ball from one end of the field to the other, with one team trying not to let the other do that.

She became interested. She flinched when they hit hard, but when Roberta leaned forward, waved her casted hand and yelled "Get him!" Graham knew football players were off the "endangered" list.

Although his team lost, Graham had a glow of satisfaction and good fellowship, having shared the game with such an enthusiastic participant. He smiled at her and opened his mouth to speak—

She exclaimed, "Good gravy! Look at the time! The whole afternoon is shot. I have to clean this place."

He looked around in astonishment. "It looks fine. How can you clean one-handed?"

"It's not impossible. My mother was adamant— once a week, you clean."

In a tone that denoted he'd thought his mother was the only one of her kind, he said, "I have a mother like that."

"There've been a lot of them. But my mother made it such a gentle admonition that there's no shaking it off without one horrific guilt trip."

Graham nodded, understanding exactly. "I didn't get ulcers."

Impressed, Roberta guessed, "You rebelled?"

He nodded solemnly. "I once didn't change the sheets for three weeks."

She laughed delightfully, and he got to watch that. Then she said, "I'm still suffering from guilt complexes."

"As an older man, I can assure you that after that initial rebellion, you go right back into the rut your mother carved for you. You're a little late. Most kids get the rebel part over with in college."

"I not only had my mother, but my sister Tate. She's a strong woman. So strong and so innovative that I became an overachiever."

"You hated her."

"Tate? Of course not. She's a fabulous woman. She just inspires you to do your best. A little better than your best."

He stood up and looked around the apartment. "What all do you want me to do?"

"I really didn't mean for you to help, not this time. We'll rotate weeks. Kitchen and dining area versus living room and porch. Since you just moved in, you're free this weekend. Of course, you do your own room and bath—" she laughed a little "—and change your sheets."

He loved it that they could laugh together and he watched her with great pleasure. With her hand in the cast, he couldn't allow her to work alone. He scrubbed out the kitchen and moved all the furniture for her to vacuum behind, before putting things back into place.

When they had finished, she smiled her ethereally magic smile and said, "You've made it so easy. Thank you. I'll fix supper for you."

"Let's go out and walk along the stream, and I'll treat us to hamburgers."

She agreed. "If we make it Dutch and split the bill."

"I eat more. We'll just pay for our own."

"Okay." It was a soft word.

She wasn't chatty. They walked in peace. That was the only word Graham could think of to describe the mood they shared. It wasn't bad, but he wanted the feeling between them to be as vibrant and exciting as what he felt inside his body. It seemed to him that every nerve and cell he had was affected by her. It was more than sexual attraction. It was something special, an awareness that shivered and quivered around in him and made him exquisitely conscious of her.

But she treated him almost as if... as if he was...as if he was a non-male. That made him a little indignant. He wanted her to realize he was a potent man. One who had designs on her. Not a threat but a treat. He wanted her giggly and flirting. Instead she walked along, looking around, pretty much as if she was alone. It was just a tad insulting to his male ego.

After supper she said good-night and went through her impregnable door and closed it. He tried to tempt her with a film on his marvelous giant screen, but she shook her head. "I've some reading to do." And she'd vanished through the portal into never-never land.

On Monday Graham began a routine he unconsciously continued. He would have done it for anyone without any undue thought, because he was a considerate man. He fixed Roberta's coffee and left it hot for her each morning thereafter.

Having the coffee already made threw her schedule off kilter. There was a time slot for each move in the morning, when she was functioning on automatic, and she found herself in the kitchen looking at a completed segment. That was disruptive. Then she had to *think* to the next step in her preparation for the day.

She was late for the bus and late to work, all because her new apartmentmate was considerate. She rushed around on appointments, checking on legislation that was in progress—legislation about pesticides and reforestation, and about groundwater and dead lakes, and about conflicts of interests between human wants and nature's needs. It was a long, slow process—one that had to be carefully, constantly monitored.

Graham arrived at his building, and he felt a little strange-dog stiff-legged at the idea of seeing Jim McFarland, who had seen Roberta Lambert...first. Jim was nowhere around.

So Graham was deep in the files on a case of a man who had ripped off the government for just a trifle more than one hundred million dollars, when Jim came into his office.

Graham had been braced and was ready to be a little protective of his newly established territory, Roberta.

Jim sat on the edge of Graham's desk and didn't look at him. "Have you moved in?"

Graham closed the file and stood up. "Yes."

"Is she...all right?"

Graham was really very kindhearted. Instead of something flippant, he simply replied, "Yes."

"Take care of her."

Softly Graham observed, "She looks like a natural wonder who ought to be preserved."

It was Jim's turn to say a sober "Yes."

"Have you...have you really given her up?"

Quietly, Jim replied, "Yes."

And with careful words carefully said, Graham told his friend, "This is your last chance to change your mind. Do you understand? This is it."

"I know."

"She treats me like a non-male." He gave Jim that comfort.

Jim looked down at his shoes. "She's so interested in saving what's left of the world that she doesn't notice men."

"Doesn't she date at all?"

"She runs around to all those fund-raisers and cocktail parties in order to say two words to some congressman on a vital committee. She doesn't have time for dates."

"How am I going to attract her attention?"

Jim looked at him. "I gave her to you. Don't expect me to help you win her!"

"Jim . . ." Graham moved his hands out helplessly.

Jim looked away. "I may not be able to dance at your wedding, but I'll be godfather to your first." Then he walked away.

Graham rubbed his face with hard hands. He went to stand at the window and look out over the gloomy pocket park with its shrubbery, bench and statue. How could he freely accept Roberta's love when Jim had wanted her so badly?

Graham thought, well, for one thing, if he wanted her love, first he had to attract her attention. In order to win her love, she had to at least know he was a person. Right now, she couldn't even see him as a man, much less as a lover. How does a man attract a woman? He'd never had that problem before now. There must be some good advice on maneuvers.

Across from the Capitol building, next to the Supreme Court building is the Library of Congress with a copy of every book imaginable. Graham spent his noon hour there, and he was stunned at all the literature on just that subject. Attracting the opposite sex had to be a problem, or there wouldn't be so much about it. He asked the librarian which book was the best one.

She stared.

He said he needed help.

She blinked and continued to stare.

He frowned at her and asked, "Which book will help me with a woman who doesn't realize I'm a healthy male?"

She looked down his body and back up. Then she shook her head just a little slowly as she suggested, "Try me."

"Well, that might be nice, but I'm in love with this woman, and it wouldn't be fair to you if I was interested in another."

She reluctantly suggested two books. She would send them over to the Justice Department library where he could check them out. She did that, and the next day he got the books. He put them into a plain brown paper sack and carried them back to the office. All afternoon he was aware of the books pulsing in his bottom desk drawer, filled with helpful ideas, and of his wanting to begin.

He went home after work and found a note on the kitchen counter saying, "I have one of the big fund-raiser dinners tonight."

That note pleased Graham inordinately. She was reporting her whereabouts. After a three-mile jog, he made himself a cheese sandwich with lettuce and pickles, and drank a beer. He looked around at the clean apartment and was contented: she had left him a note.

He took those two books into his room. He played his phone tape and returned a couple of calls. Then he lay on the bed to learn how to become clever about women. The books were well-worn, so they had had more than their share of attention.

One was very basic. It said to bathe and wear clean clothing. He skipped down to "Become interested in what interests her/him."

He snapped the book closed and went into the living room to look over the bookcase. There were all those books. He took *Silent Spring* from the shelf and carried it back into his room. He opened it and began to read.

Being a speed reader, he finished the book at 9:42 p.m. He looked at the clock and was startled. Roberta should be home any minute. He'd just made it into the living room and turned on the TV when Roberta's key sounded in the lock. She was home.

He tried to smile casually. Although he did rise to greet her, he stayed where he was until she came closer. Then he reached, with slow masculine movements, to easily help her with her coat.

She allowed that, maneuvering her cast out of the sleeve as she watched the screen. She said with delight, "I remember that one. It's good." During commercials they made snacks, and it was almost eleven when she said an airy "'Night," and disappeared through that door of hers.

He saw her only briefly during that week. When she came home, she bravely walked past the TV with her face averted and her cast blocking her vision. She said staunchly, "I can't stay up late."

There was no football game on Saturday. He told her the TV was riddled with basketball. Roberta squinted at Graham as she inquired, "Riddled? How can a Hoosier use such a word about basketball?"

He replied logically, "It's not football."

She had office work to catch up on and was gone all day. Graham was restless with both football *and* Roberta missing from his life. He called some friends and went out into the countryside to jog and have lunch before returning to her apartment. His apartment.

She came home tired, pale and droopy. With a vague greeting and a half wave, she went on through and vanished into her room.

On Sunday, she'd left before he even awakened, and it was noon before she returned. He heard her at the door and went to meet her in the roar of the game on TV.

He hung her coat away in the closet as she asked, "What's happening?"

He wasn't sure, so he said, "They're trying for a first down." Since they were always trying for a first down, it seemed safe to say.

During a commercial, she ran to her door and slipped away. After a time, she returned in a pink velvet lounge suit that was as soft and clingy as the blue one had been, and she was wiping cream from her face again, just like before. She sat on the edge of her sofa cushion and asked, "Who's playing?"

He was astonished that he remembered. He was wondering how to prevent her from buying a large screen of her own and setting it up in that hidden lair of hers. Mentally he short-circuited selected portions of the electrical plugs in her never-never land.

They made lunch at halftime, bringing their plates and glasses to the table by the sofa. And they argued about which team was doing what right, and he told her she was crazy and that she was out in . . . left field. She loved it and laughed deliciously.

The afternoon wore on in the lopsided game, and during another commercial, she went into the kitchen and returned with a cache of goodies she'd brought home, in her purse, from the Friday-night party. "I know the caterer, and she gave me these. Try this one. You get only one of those. Isn't it delicious? No! You can't have that last one, that's mine. Here, you can have this instead. Do you like anchovies?"

He was charmed by her, but she was treating him as she would a brother. That wasn't what he wanted. He wanted her to fall back against the doorjamb and half faint at the sight of him. And here she was, sharing goodies she'd brought home in her purse. Well, maybe that was a beginning.

Three

Graham's mother had always told him that learning anything worthwhile took time. That was mostly said when he had to practice on the piano. It had been his decision not to play for a year in high school, but then he found that being able to play the piano was a free ticket to lots of parties, and that girls hung around piano players. They hung around saxophone players, too, but while playing the piano, a guy could talk, smile and ask for phone numbers. He doubted his mother had had woman-snaring in mind when she'd insisted that he learn. It was only after playing voluntarily that he realized how much he loved music and that it took time to play well.

Besides learning to play a piano, getting Roberta Lambert's attention was taking a long time. She wasn't around very much, for one thing, and her evenings were almost always taken up with fund-raisers. The book said one of the primary ways to court a woman was to give her a good time: "Wine and dine."

And flowers.

The first time he brought flowers home, on a dreary January day, she was gone. There was another of her notes, and this one said, "I have to go to Nevada about contaminated soil. Would you please ask Maintenance to look at the garbage disposal? Be back Thursday. Bob."

But he wasn't going to call her Bob. He would call her Roberta. It would remind her that she was a woman, and that he was a man.

The books said, "Admire her/his good points." And Graham surely did. Yes, he did admire Roberta's good points—all of them.

And in the section of advice specifically for men, it said, "Help her. Lift and carry things. Protect her. See to her comfort." She had to be around for him to do that, and she was out in Nevada where all the cowboys were hustling her. Everybody knew about cowboys. They didn't have to read "how-to" books on women. Damn.

It was at lunch a day or so later, in the cafeteria, that Graham was given his first brilliant idea for his assault on Roberta's gratitude.

While eating lunch with his cohorts, one of the women was saying, "—big as a horse! It came across the floor with the speed of light, and I screamed! Of course, since I live alone, there was no one else there. I got on the kitchen table and reached across the Grand Canyon to the phone and called Maintenance. They were placidly kind and after a while, one came over with traps. I inquired, 'Just who is going to empty those traps?' And he looked at me and took a steadying breath before he replied earnestly, 'Just call.' You can tell jobs are hard to find or he would have said, 'Lady, you know what you can do with them traps?' ''

A brilliant light illuminated Graham's brain and a deep voice said inside his head, "A mouse. She's talking about a mouse."

It isn't easy to buy a gray mouse in Washington, D.C. The guy at the pet shop asked, "What you want a gray one for? We got white ones. You can get gray ones a dime a dozen."

But you couldn't. And Roberta would suspect a white mouse wasn't a real threat. White mice are generally pets. That evening he sauntered over to Maintenance and enquired casually, "You have many mice around?"

"Naw, the buildings are built tight. And we got Buttercup. We lend him around to anybody wants him."

"Buttercup?"

"A cat."

Graham nodded thoughtfully.

He finally paid a street kid five dollars to catch a healthy mouse for him. Graham supplied the cage. It had a round floor and a wire dome. The kid squinted at Graham and kept his distance. Graham explained, "It's for a woman I know." And the kid laughed fit to split. Graham smiled. The kid was still young. He had a lot to learn about women.

So two days later Graham had a live, gray mouse. There were five other kids who watched the exchange of cage with mouse for *five dollars*. And there was some vocal campaigning for Graham to have more mice. "A friend for 'im. He'll be lonesome all by himself.'' Graham figured that kid would do all right in the years ahead. He was a hustler.

Graham drove home with the caged mouse sitting beside him on the front seat. The mouse was looking around and sniffing, very curious. God only knew where all that mouse had been and with whom. It could be riddled with diseases and fleas. Graham couldn't introduce fleas and disease into Roberta's scrubbed apartment. He took the mouse to a veterinarian.

The woman receptionist looked at the mouse and then at Graham and inquired, ''You want a bath and shots for a gray mouse?''

''Please.''

She excused herself courteously and went into another room. The people sitting along the wall watched Graham. He knew it was nothing personal, since people who were bored tended to watch anything that moved. Idle eyes needed something to do.

The vet came out with the receptionist. The vet nodded to Graham and picked up the cage to look at the mouse. She said, ''All right. Give the information to Sheila and wait your turn.'' Then she exited through the door.

Sheila asked, ''Name?''

''Graham Rawlins.''

''The mouse.''

''Uh ... Gus.'' Graham had always liked the fat little mouse in Disney's *Cinderella*, and his name had been Gus.

She wrote ''Gus.'' Then she inquired about other pertinent facts before saying ''Be seated. We take people 'first come, first served.' ''

Graham sat with his caged mouse on his lap and looked at the other pets. The dogs and cats were inter-

ested. The parrot wasn't. The creatures' slaves were.
After a time one said, "That a pedigree?" And he
laughed. "Har, har, har,"

Graham smiled and said kindly, "No."

The grinning man nodded once and no one said
anything else.

A young woman came in with a parakeet that was
saying "Damn" a lot, and it was obvious it felt that
way. The woman was cheerful and inquired of Graham, "I don't believe I've ever seen a gray mouse in
captivity. Why did you cage it?"

"I'm going to rescue a woman from it."

She laughed, and then some of the men began to
laugh. But some of the women were appalled: "How
could you?"

But the men thought that was a great idea. One
asked slyly, "Having a little trouble getting her attention?"

So he, at least, understood.

Several of the women, including the receptionist,
then looked at Graham in a different way. One finally
asked, "She isn't interested?"

Candidly, and because he knew that one solicits advice on any problem, he replied, "She doesn't realize
I'm a man."

That broke up the whole room.

"So you're going to let the mouse out, and she'll
scream, and you'll rescue her. Not bad." That rejoin-
der was from a man.

An older lady—with a fat, blinking cat—put in her
oar with "Men!"

Graham angled for sympathy. "I've tried about
everything else. She's so busy, I hardly ever see her, and

she's thinking about everything but me." He thought of the situation as being a little like group therapy.

One woman said, "Get sick." And another said, "Ask her advice." But a man said, "Before you get sick, try the mouse." "There'll probably be a run on mice. Get that? A run on mice. Mouse run?"

It fell a little flat, but Graham was courteous and smiled with a saluting nod.

Then began a round of suggestions. Most were in the book, but Graham listened to them all, because one never knew when some valuable tip would turn up. The final consensus was that the mouse might do the trick.

As the discussion went on, some of the patients had to be carried away into the doctor's office, and new ones arrived. The new arrivals' slaves were brought up-to-date on the discussion and some entered in, while others just stared.

It finally came time for Gus to be seen, and Graham thanked those present for being helpful, before he carried Gus into the examination room.

The vet was businesslike. "Is this a pet?"

"No, I bought it off a street kid. I'm going to give it to a woman I know, who isn't paying any attention to me."

The vet gave him a brief look. Then wearing protective gloves, she took the mouse out of the cage and examined it. "It's a male." She bathed it and sprayed it with an insect repellent, rubbing it in. The mouse didn't appear to mind. She gave it a shot in its tail and said, "You'll need some food pellets and water. See Sheila." Then she smiled a little and added, "Good luck."

With the initial investment of five dollars for acquisition and a seven-fifty cage, when Graham left the vet's office he had just over fifty dollars tied up in that mouse.

It was a male. Good thing it was, since he'd named it Gus without knowing that. Having it *male* made it seem more of an entity, less anonymous. A coconspirator?

In the car, Graham looked over to the cage on the other seat where the mouse was cleaning his whiskers. "You must think the world's gone crazy. There you were, running from hungry cats and trying to find something to eat, and now here you are—bathed, inoculated, with a dish of free food, *nutritionally balanced*. You're a lucky rodent. All you have to do is play your part when the time comes. Scare the liver out of Roberta, and your entire life will not have been in vain."

Stuck at a traffic light, Graham watched as the mouse cautiously approached the clever, unspillable dish of pellets. Its nose didn't smell anything exciting and the mouse left the dish.

"I should have asked how old you are. You're acting like a juvenile who'll only eat hamburgers and malts when you could have flounder and vegetables. Get hungry, Gus; you don't know what's good for you."

At the apartment complex, Graham had to make two trips from the parking lot. He wrapped the cage in a sweatshirt from the trunk of his car. It was somewhat cold for his fifty-dollar investment, and he couldn't risk anyone seeing him carrying a mouse inside. Then he went back for the jugged water and the pellet sack. It weighed ten pounds. A rip-off. A mouse would take a year to eat all that food, but it was the smallest amount they'd had.

He put Gus in a corner of his room and stored the food and water in the bottom of the linen closet. Brushing his hands together, he smiled. He was ready.

Then he lay on his bed and fantasized about the scenario. He'd let Gus out, Gus would scamper across the kitchen floor, Roberta would see the mouse and scream, and Graham would arrive. Roberta would fling herself into his arms . . . and become aware of him as a man. He'd be naked, she would soon be, too, and they'd fall to the floor and make love.

Sure.

Well, he'd comfort her, telling her he was there and she was safe, and she'd be grateful. It was Tuesday. She'd be home on Thursday. He might have to wait a day or two until the situation was just right. Sunday was the Super Bowl. They'd have all the rest of the evening for him to comfort her and make her feel protected.

Protected.

He went to a drugstore and bought some protection for her.

On Wednesday he was told one of the other attorneys couldn't do a deposition in Georgia and would Graham please get to it? In plain words, he knew that meant he was to get himself down to Georgia, as soon as possible. He smiled and said he'd be honored.

He was to be gone two days. He went home to pack and told Gus he'd be back in plenty of time. And he put a good three-day supply of pellets and water in Gus's nonspillable dishes.

The deposition took four days instead of two. Graham called and left a message on Roberta's answering machine. He'd written it out, and practiced it so that it wouldn't sound dumb, and he read it quite easily. But he ended with an extraneous and husky "Take care," followed by a long pause in which he tried to think of a way to erase the two betraying words. Then he said briskly, "Graham."

Just such careless words from an unguarded tongue could put her on her guard. What a klutz he was. He didn't deserve her. Oh, yes, he did.

It wasn't until the next morning when he rolled out of bed and stared into the hotel's empty corner that he remembered in the corner of his bedroom back home was a mouse who depended on him.

He could hardly call Roberta on Friday and say, "Uh, would you mind feeding my mouse?" That would blow the whole ball of wax. So when the deposition proved so fruitfully advantageous for their case and needed more time, Graham paid his own way home in order to feed that damned mouse whose cost now amounted to two hundred and fifty dollars. Well, Roberta was worth it. And this just might be the time to use the mouse.

It was no surprise when he didn't find Roberta at home. Gus stood up on his hind legs and wiggled his nose. He had plenty of food and more than an ample supply of water. "You're a hell of a lot of trouble. You'd better do your share when the time comes. Understand?"

He cleaned the whole apartment, waiting for Roberta. She didn't show up until after ten. She was holding her cast together with the other hand, *and she'd been crying*.

He was sitting in the dark living room and on the giant screen the movie had come to a part that was a tense and silent stalking, so there had been no sound in the apartment. When Graham saw that Roberta had been crying, he got up off the sofa in alarm, and she shrieked!

He took her shoulders and snarled, "Are you hurt?"

She questioned, "Graham?"

"Yes!" he hissed through his teeth. "What's the matter?"

"You're hurting my arms."

"Oh, sorry." He let go of her, but he didn't move away and stood looming over her.

"You scared the beejeebers out of me. I thought you were down in Georgia."

"Why were you crying?"

"Some guy got off the bus with me and wouldn't bug off, so I swung my cast at him and it broke."

"What guy?"

"Security chased him, but I think he got away."

"Security?"

"They watch for me at night when I get off the bus. If I'm later than eleven, I take a cab."

"Your hand hurts?"

"It's not quite healed. I just came in to change clothes and go to the hospital to get it fixed. I'll call a cab."

"Not with me here. And you're fine the way you're dressed."

She was wearing a sparkly red dress, and the high heels brought her mouth up within better range of his. The wind had loosened her hair, and it gave her a casual, careless abandoned look. He said, "Want to just let your hair down?"

"I suppose. What are you doing home?"

"I came home—" and the word was sweet to say to her "—because..." He couldn't possibly say it was to see her. "I had some things that I had to do." Like feed the mouse that was going to cause Roberta Lambert to jump into his arms.

Her left hand searched around in her hair for pins. Then, in the slow motion of important happenings that are impossible but which really occur, he lifted his hands and his voice said, far-off in the distance, "Let me."

Her hand dropped down, and she stood obediently. He had to search carefully, and her hair was silk to his clumsy rough, fingers. His hands made love to her head, to the silken strands that covered it, and to her— although she didn't realise it.

Very seriously, he put his hand under her chin and gently tilted it up so that he could prolong the nearness. He saw the tears on her cheeks and his heart squeezed. Very tenderly, he brushed the tears away with one awkward finger that smeared her makeup. "Did he frighten you badly?"

"Him? Of course not. My hand hurts."

That she hadn't been frightened startled him a bit. Then he understood that she hurt, and he was very gentle. But he released her in order to put on his shoes.

She was twenty-nine years old and knew enough about makeup to know that while it could withstand a tear or two, it could never survive a man's fingers. So as he went to the closet for a raincoat, she dug into her pocket and pulled out a tissue to wipe her cheeks.

They left the apartment, leaving the television on and her purse lying on the sofa.

Going through the emergency entrance at the hospital, they were prepared to wait an interminable time, and Graham anticipated the closeness that would engender.

He noted they were given rather penetrating glances, especially by the guard. Graham was unshaven and his blond hair was tousled. He was in dark jeans and a dark T-shirt, and his raincoat had never received any real consideration. He looked like a mugger, and Roberta looked like his victim.

Her bone doctor just happened to be there because of an automobile wreck, and he was through with that patient and ready to leave. He smiled and greeted Roberta, remembering her vividly. How many specialists remembered patients referred only for casts? Graham watched him like a hawk.

The doctor asked Roberta, "What happened?"

"A masher."

"Him?" He tilted his head at Graham.

She replied, "Of course not."

And Graham went along to watch the broken cast removed and a new one formed. He went because he wouldn't let go of Roberta's other arm. When a nurse tried to detach him, Graham told her, "Don't do that."

Falsely welcoming, the doctor asked Graham, "Would you like to watch?"

Graham gave a single, abrupt nod.

With a sharing of humor, the doctor asked Roberta, "Is he a nuisance?"

And Roberta said stiffly, "He's protective."

Thrills soared though Graham. She was defending him to the doctor! She was snubbing the doctor for poking fun at his wanting to be with her. *There was hope!*

Well. Maybe. Maybe she just didn't like anyone putting anyone else down. She was an environmentalist, and she might look on him as being some peculiar specimen who was endangered. Even the ugly condor was agonized over. This wasn't the time to feel secure.

But he held her other hand, and while the doctor and nurse released her poor semihealed hand from the remnants of the ruined cast, Graham put her well hand against his chest. He held it there with one of his big hands to give her his strength. He put his other hand on the back of her shoulders so that his thumb was on one side of her nape and his long fingers reached clear over onto her other shoulder. He knew he must appear possessive as he frowned at the doctor's hands, which *had* to examine the damage. And Roberta's wince went through Graham's body like lightning bolts.

The doctor pronounced, "I think it's okay. But we'll need a picture, just to be sure." He cocked an eyebrow at Graham. "Are you going to wait here? Or do we need to give you protective covering?" It was late, and he was tired, so he was a little snide.

Graham gave him his sharing smile.

The doctor chuckled.

Roberta heard the male-sharing in the sound and frowned. She felt she'd missed something. But the nurse was grinning, too, and she was urging Roberta to go for the X ray.

The nurse asked one personal question. "You sure it wasn't him that broke that cast?"

Roberta's words were sure. "It was not."

So that meant the nurse had to ask another. "How come you're all dressed up, and he isn't even shaved? You want to go out, and he wouldn't?"

"I got off the bus and some guy got off with me. Security at the apartment watches for me and interrupted him, but I'd already clobbered the guy with the cast."

"There was blood on it."

"I aimed for his nose."

The nurse laughed. "Mark up one for our side."

Roberta returned the smile.

"That man out there waiting for you is something."

"Do you think so?"

"How about giving him my phone number?"

"No."

And the nurse laughed softly. It was the kind of laugh that was very similar to the male exchange between the doctor and Graham. Both women heard it, and then Roberta understood the look between the men.

Since Roberta didn't have her purse, Graham paid the bill. She fretted over that. He said he'd take it off his rent, and she thought that would be okay. But it had pleased him to pay her bill. It had touched a satisfaction in him to do that simple thing for her.

The trip to hospital had taken several hours and when they returned to the apartment, Roberta looked worn out. Graham didn't want to have her away from him. He told her to change and come back, that he'd fix her some cocoa.

She said, "I'm too tired, and since you were driving, they gave me a pill at the hospital. It's made me feel as if I'm not in touch. I'll say good-night. And, Graham, thank you." She stood for a minute just looking at him, before she turned away to go to her room.

He solemnly watched her leave him and go through the alluring doorway to disappear. She'd called him by name. Come to think of it, she'd said his name when she'd come home earlier. His mind had registered it, to cherish it later. And now she'd done it again.

His name said twice did not an affair make. Everybody said names. There was nothing unusual about her calling him by his name. He was getting strange. They'd thought so at the hospital, too. They'd thought he was a mugger. What mugger had ever taken his victim to the hospital? Graham Rawlins was no mugger. He was a good man.

He turned out the lights and turned off the television. He went into his room and stripped. He longed to go and get into bed with her and hold her in his arms to keep her safe. She probably wouldn't understand. If he went and got into her bed, naked, she'd probably jump to the wrong conclusions as to why he was there. She'd probably jump, all right—right out of bed. She'd yell bloody murder.

He took a long, hot shower and dried off his weary, restless body. To relax, he took an aspirin and sat on the edge of his bed to see that Gus was awake, too. "We can't do it tomorrow," Graham informed the mouse. "We have to wait until she's recovered from tonight. I hope you're not getting impatient."

The mouse didn't reply.

Graham assured Gus, "She's worth the inconvenience."

The mouse washed his face and groomed his generous whiskers.

Graham turned off the lights and lay down. Then he got up and wrote on a piece of paper, "I cleaned." He thought of a great deal he could add and a great many signatures, but he only added a *G*. That could stand for "Gus." He smiled. But she didn't know about Gus. He carried the paper out to the kitchen and put it by the coffeepot.

It was just a good thing he remembered to do that, because the apartment was so clean that she'd never notice she was cleaning cleaned rooms. Maybe she was stringent about cleaning because, environmentally, her apartment was one thing she could control.

When he woke up Saturday, it was after eight. He lay there, discouraged. He'd hoped this weekend would be a turning point. But with her having been attacked like that, she'd be even more leery of men. Damn that guy!

He got up and spoke courteously to Gus, who wiggled his nose. The mouse was eating a pellet. Graham sympathized that starvation drove males to doing all sorts of desperate things. Starved for attention yesterday, he'd needlessly cleaned a clean apartment. He rinsed off in the shower and pulled on fresh clothes. Doing so was in the book.

He went out, barefoot, and needing a shave, to see if there was any coffee. The maker was clean, and his note was still there. She was still asleep? He frowned. Then he called the hospital and asked what kind of pill they'd given Miss Lambert last night and how long would she sleep.

After a while the woman came back on the phone and said, "If she isn't awake by four o'clock, stimulate her."

"*Stimulate?* Just what did you have in mind?"

The woman laughed and said, "Tickle the bottom of her foot. If she reacts, she's fine. She was tired and had been under stress. She can use the sleep."

"How about 'stimulating' her now, just to be sure?"

"She might not have had enough rest. Give her time. She's a little run-down anyway. She needs the sleep."

He thanked the nurse and hung up the phone. If Roberta didn't awaken by four, he would knock on that door. He might even turn the knob and go inside her retreat. He was torn between wanting her awake and wanting a reason to go in and see her asleep. To stand and fill his soul by just looking at her. Life is really disturbing, he decided, with choices and problems and women.

He wasn't unreasonably noisy as he fixed an enormous breakfast. But he wasn't quiet, either. Even with all the people he saw and talked to, he was lonesome; that's what he was. He'd been most of the week without seeing her. Then, when he did, she was in distress. And now she was asleep, out of reach beyond that door.

He cleaned his own room, changed the sheets and took all his things to the laundry. He never did his own. He gave it all to the attendant and let her figure it out. But he dropped by Security and inquired about the encounter Roberta had had the night before.

The man on duty was Graham's father's age. He told Graham rather coolly that they'd caught the guy, and he'd been warned. The guy's nose had been bloodied. He'd only been annoyingly persistent in wanting to know Roberta. He hadn't harmed her. He'd been a little drunk. When he'd sobered up, he was released. He'd be a careful man from then on out.

"How can you tell that?"

"You learn people. What are your intentions?"

"Honorable."

"Behave."

Graham was a little offended.

He went back and told Gus the whole episode. Then he scanned his books again on how to entice a woman. They said to smile and not to be forward. He rubbed his chest and groaned. They said to be gentlemanly and watch his language. And they told about manners.

He went back to sleep. Roberta wasn't the only one who was wrung out.

He'd left his door open, so he heard her close the refrigerator door. He opened his eyes, knowing something important was happening. He'd been sleeping so hard that, for a minute, he didn't even know where he was, much less why he was waiting to hear something. He sat up and recognized that he was in his room at the apartment, and Gus made a musical sound. Rather amazed, Graham looked at the mouse.

Then he got up and rubbed his face, which made him realize that he still hadn't shaved. He went into his small hall, closing his bedroom door, and looked out into the living room. She was fixing breakfast in the kitchen.

He went into the bathroom and shaved very carefully. Then he went out to her. She was at the table, eating, and she smiled at him.

She smiled! The sun came out on that miserable day, and he smiled back. "How're you doing?"

"I'm as good as new."

"Good."

"Thank you for cleaning."

"I didn't have anything to do, and there wasn't a football game to be found."

She laughed a throaty sound that sent shivers through his body and tickled each of his hair roots all over his skin's surface. It was erotically stunning. He stood braced against the invisible onslaught as she asked, "Are you having lunch? Or will you join me for breakfast?"

Being automatically honest, he replied, "Lunch."

She started to rise.

She meant to fix his lunch! "No. I'll just have a cheese sandwich. And a beer. I'll just be a minute. My, but you were hungry. Does battle stir your appetite?" Good Lord, why had he said that? Now she'd remember and be alarmed and fearful and—

"Yes." She looked wicked. "I've become very good at squashing noses."

"A Carry Nation of the mashers?"

She lifted her coffee cup to salute him. "Great wordage."

"How's the hand?"

"A little tender, but not as bad as when I broke it on that first guy's nose."

"When did you confront that purse snatcher?"

"Just before Christmas. It's a Coach purse and precious to me, but even more important, I had my list of all the family's clothes sizes. Think of shopping without that! It fairly boggles the mind."

And he smiled. Maybe he wouldn't need Gus after all.

They ate together, but she wasn't chatty. She seemed peaceful, calm, and oddly contented. He decided it had to be the sleeping pill. She was still somewhat sedated.

He'd lost his chance to get past that door to view her private kingdom, tickle her foot . . . and stimulate her.

Four

With Roberta still semi-sedated from the sleeping pill and the apartment already cleaned, the two semi-strangers lingered over breakfast, getting acquainted. They spoke of their families and where they'd gone to school, and began the tentative sharing of their lives, their views and their ideals.

The widening of their acquaintance pleased Graham, and he smiled at Roberta, considering her. Finally he said, "It must be tough trying to change sheets with that cast. I could do it for you, unless you're in the middle of a three-week rebellion." Graham couldn't prevent a small grin.

Roberta gave one nod to acknowledge the shared humor. "I struggled through sheet-changing yesterday. I do have to take the load over to the laundry. If you're going over, would you take mine, too?"

"No problem." He nicely sidestepped the fact he'd already done that. "Any errands? Groceries?"

"I'm stocked. Want to share a stew? I'm going to dump one into the slow cooker."

"'Dump.'" He tasted that word as applied to cooking and serving food by a purported nest builder.

She laughed outright. "I didn't want you to think I was enticing you with a meal."

He didn't know how to respond to that. Could he beg to be enticed? What did the book say? How could he excuse himself while he went to look up replies? He said, "I don't think any woman has ever *tried* to entice me. How does it work? How does a man recognize enticement?"

She bubbled with unbelieving laughter. It was a lovely sound to his ears, and he watched her with attention. She gasped, "No woman has... Yeah. You want to sell me lake property in New Mexico, right?"

"Honey—" since his tone was just right, she wouldn't notice him calling her honey, and he savored saying the word "—you have to know that I don't know one thing about women. Really! I mean it! Come on, now, settle down and listen to me. I played football all through high school and college, and I was pro for two very banged-up years. Since we didn't have a daddy, and mother was raising us seven kids by herself, there were zero funds for college, and law school was out of the question. I had to struggle, or be in debt all my natural life or pledge my firstborn child. The only woman I really know is my mother, and she's a no-nonsense, hard-nosed disciplinarian who loved us all enormously and thought we were perfect—as soon as the rough edges had been smoothed. I had to study, work, work out, and play the piano."

"So—" But she stopped. Then she started again and said, "So you play the piano?"

"Brilliantly." He gave her a modest look. "That's why I've never been enticed. Women come and sit by piano players and say hello. Right out. I've never been lured. How does a woman do that? With a stew dumped into a pot? That doesn't sound too enticing."

"She doesn't *tell* him she's dumped it. She serves it nicely and smiles."

"Sorta showing off what he can expect?"

"Yes."

"I'm a pretty good cook. I wouldn't mind if a woman couldn't."

"That blows all the rules." She shook her head chidingly. "The way to a man's heart is through his stomach. If you don't need someone to cook for you, what's left?" She'd started out sassily logical, but as soon as the words were out, her eyes filled with laughter. She struggled not to laugh, but she blushed scarlet.

She wasn't any more practiced than he! How astonishing. He lowered his eyelids halfway and said, "I suppose she'd have to think of something else." He paused tellingly before he added, "Like changing his sheets and cleaning his shoes?"

"Then if I make the Lambert-family Texas biscuits, you won't assume I'm enticing you?"

He had to lick his lips. "I'll just think you're hungry for your mother's biscuits. Are you any good at making them? Or will I be forced to risk my teeth by eating two just to be polite and not hurt your feelings?"

Her look could easily have been called tender. "You need only commit to one, but you may not eat more than half. Understand? And I stole a jar of my sister Georgine's kumquat jam at Christmas, and you can only have a single spoonful of that.''

"Rules." He spoke as if disgruntled, but he watched her, his eyes caressing her. "I like those soft lounge suits you wear.''

"Dressing is a nuisance with this cast. I bought these to solve some of it.''

He gave her a bland look. "I'd be glad to help in any way I can. Roomies pitch in, in emergencies. I'm up a half hour before you, and it wouldn't be any trouble for me to help you dress.''

"You're all heart.''

He gave a thoughtful glance down her body. "Offhand, I would bet panty hose are hard to put on single-handed.''

"You win. They are.''

"Remember: anytime.''

"No way.''

He was astonished. "I'm just trying to help.''

She gave him a scoffing grin and got up, taking her dishes to the sink.

As they cleaned up after themselves, working in good harmony, she asked, "What sort of football did you play?''

"I was the only one awed that I would be on the field, and I thought everything I managed to do was remarkable. The coach thought I was mediocre. I played for the Indianapolis Colts, and I was an unappreciated striver. Once I dropped the ball, and the coach, who was a sour man, said he guessed I wasn't any better than nothing at all.''

"How cruel.''

"When I intercepted a pass—that's when it's the other team's ball, do you know that? I did that, and I expected the coach to celebrate, but he only snarled, 'Why didn't you run?' He hadn't even noticed that five of the enemy were wrapped around my legs and piled on my body." Graham sighed. "As soon as I had enough to get me through law school, I quit." He'd also paid off his siblings' school debts.

"The coaches didn't coax you to stay longer?"

"Nope. They even threw a party and celebrated me leaving. Everybody came, and they all laughed and were cheerful."

"You miss it."

"In agony," he agreed.

She grinned.

But she didn't touch him. She avoided contact. He tried, but she seemed to anticipate touching and avoided it. Was she repulsed by him? Or was she just used to keeping to herself?

He would need Gus.

They went into the living room and sat down. He told her, "Tomorrow is the Super Bowl. Do you realize that? If you have nothing else to do, then let's make a party of it. I'll get Coney dogs and beer, and we'll have popcorn and ice cream. How's that?"

"Okay."

She didn't sound very excited about it. "You do know that this is the ultimate for the year? The whole pro season climaxes tomorrow. The two best teams meet, and it's a challenge to the greatest of the Titans' clashes."

"I'm not sure I trust your evaluation of this. Oddly enough, no parties are slated for tomorrow, so I am free. I'll try it, for a while."

"You're a natural for football. I heard you yelling when you watched with me a couple of weeks ago. You're a fighter. And that cast on your hand will make you feel like one of the guys. They're all in bandages and casts. I wore a fake one once just to feel like part of the team. I was warming the bench. That means I wasn't needed to play, you see, and I was feeling out of it."

Her smile lingered as her eyes rested on him for longer than usual.

"You don't have plans tonight, do you?"

She shook her head.

"Good. Tell me where your dirty clothes are, and I'll do any shopping you need." He stood up and started toward her door.

She scrambled after him, going around him to her door. "I'll get it. Check the popcorn. It's in the cupboard above the fridge. I don't drink beer. See if there's any wine under the sink." She disappeared through her door, and he was thwarted again.

She had some Kellercup, a squat bottle of Mogan David grape and a pink Chablis.

She was already back with her laundry neatly tied in a bundle. That quick, that organized. Well, anyone who'd clean a clean apartment would be just that tidy. He was doomed never to see that mysterious room.

He was so motivated to get back to her that the errands were quickly done. She opened the door for him, and it was such a thrill that he had to take a breath and tell his body to behave and move naturally and not to touch her—yet.

He brought in his own packaged laundry. She had to know he'd made a special trip to take hers because her eyes sparkled and she gave him another smile. But she simply accepted that it was so, and gave no protest.

She almost followed him into his hall. At the last minute he realized she was behind him, and over the thrill of that, he remembered *Gus*! So he put the package of clean laundry on the floor in his hall and closed the door against a faint trill of sound coming through his closed bedroom door.

She asked, "Did you hear something?"

He didn't ask what sound but simply said "No."

She looked at him thoughtfully.

They spent the day together in easy companionship. He wallowed in her presence. He curtailed his speech and asked her questions, and resisted expounding on his own ideas. Being rather lonely, away from his family, he did tend to talk too much. He encouraged her. "Tell me what you're doing now in your work."

"We're making up a report to mail out, telling what we've been doing. This next week is going to be hectic, stuffing and mailing."

"I thought that was done mechanically," he said.

"This way's cheaper. We have volunteers who come in and work free."

"Can you use extra people, or do you have enough?"

"We always need volunteers."

He inquired, "What's in the report?"

"We try not to be too glum. Serious enough to make people realize the problems are humongous, but not allowing any despair over them. People can be defeated just by the scope of dangerous-waste sites. But there's no other planet. We have to cope.

"This year we are cautioning people to pay attention. Every little bit hurts. Our slogan is What's What

You're Doing, Doing Downstream? It's like litter. I was at a Fourth of July parade, and people had brought chairs to sit along the street. When it was over, the nice middle-class people stood up, picked up their chairs and left a shocking mess of litter behind them. It was offensively inconsiderate."

"Not their yard," he suggested.

"It's their world. Why make a mess someone else must clean up?"

"The people you represent are lucky to have you."

"As is said, this is the only planet we have. It would be a sin to louse it up."

He nodded slowly, watching her.

They walked around the jogging path about eight times, talking, being silent, being together but apart. They went back to their apartment and had the stew from the slow cooker with the Lambert-family Texas biscuits. He had his share and then argued that he was bigger and should have more. She said no, she'd warned him about just that sort of thinking. He told her that she was a glutton.

She not only hotly denied that, she also accused him of sneaking a second spoonful of kumquat jam. He was offended and argued. She showed him how low the jam was in the jar. He said, "Sue me."

"I would, but the judge would probably have to taste the jam in order to understand the gravity of the situation, and I refuse to give up any more of the jam."

He could understand that.

They watched a double feature, and commented unkindly as it went along. The premise involved a legal issue, and the laws of the land and the routine checks had been ignored, so the plot was impossible. The second film, a tearjerker, reached too hard, and they became engrossed in an argument about something else entirely. It was exhilarating. And they tested each other's knowledge.

He stuck to his position on one question and couldn't be lured beyond the facts. She was so impressed that he had to admit that all he knew was from an article he'd read, which had made sense, so he'd winged it. She smote her forehead and was disgusted.

When midnight came, she parted from him with easy casualness and went to bed.

He waited, hoping she'd come back out again, but she didn't. He finally went into his hallway, stumbled over the packages of laundry and opened the door to his bedroom to be greeted by a trill from Gus. It really hit Graham then. The mouse could sing! He'd heard of such, but a common, street mouse? Then he wondered if Roberta had heard Gus more than that one brief time.

Graham leaned over the cage and the mouse stood on its hind legs and looked up at him. Graham said through his teeth, "Don't ruin this for me. Do you hear me?"

The mouse thrilled nicely. Graham frowned, listening. Good pitch. He put away his laundry and got ready for bed. His body was impatient and needy. He showered and brushed his teeth, frowning at himself in the mirror. He told his image, "Any other man wouldn't be sleeping alone three weeks later."

He climbed into bed, turned off the light and lay glowering at the ceiling. He went to sleep, lulled by the trilling of the mouse.

The next day, Super Bowl Sunday, he was soberly fixing eggs and bacon for breakfast when the portal opened and the goddess appeared in mortal form. He saw that that was so, and he was awed.

She said, "Good morning."

He asked, "Want some eggs and bacon?" He figured it was better to act normal than to fall to his knees and worship her.

"Perfect."

She was perfect. "Sit down and keep out of my way."

"There are four biscuits left over."

He turned and stared. "So that's why there weren't enough. You sneaked them out of my share!"

"I did not. Two from yours and two from mine."

"That's what you say, *now*."

"Cross my heart."

"You realize this is the big day?"

She was cautious. "What big day?"

"Super Bowl Sunday."

She had the audacity to grin dismissively.

"Who're you going to root for?"

"I'll see."

"We ought to bet," he said. "This is a good time to introduce you to the evils of sports betting."

"Oh?"

"How about twenty cents?"

"I'll have to check the budget."

"Now we have to decide who you're going to choose." He broke a match and aligned the pieces. "Short one gets the blues. The long one, the reds. Okay?" He held out his hand with the tips of the broken match showing between his thumb and the side of his palm.

She reached for the farthest one, but he pulled his hand back and said, "Not that one."

She was indignant. "I thought this was free choice."

"Nothing in life's free choice. It's all contrived enticement. You've told me that yourself. Take the other one."

"Why did you go through all this broken-match bit? Why didn't you just tell me which team I was supposed to back?"

He looked offended. "That would be dictatorial."

"You're impossible."

"I'm the easiest man you'll ever meet in all of your life."

"Baloney."

"That sounds as if you might not belive me."

"Are you going to invite anyone else to this...Super Bowl?"

"I hadn't thought about it."

"It's a shame to hoard that big screen. How about asking...was it Jim McFarland?"

"No."

"I thought he was a friend of yours."

"Yeah. Sorta." The words were very grudging.

"That *was* the name of the man you asked me about, wasn't it?"

"I don't remember."

"How else would I know his name?"

Graham knew her subconscious remembered when Jim had met her and begun to struggle not to fall in love with her. Jim had been smart. Strong, but smart. He'd gotten rid of the problem by tossing Roberta Lambert over into Graham's lap.... He wished she was on his lap. He looked at her.

She was watching him with great curiosity. Had she begun to remember Jim? He couldn't allow that. "I have a practice keyboard with headphones. Would you like to hear me play?"

"Do you play well?"

"Brilliantly."

"The way you played football?"

He nodded gravely. "Equally so."

She was reluctant. He waited. She said, "One piece."

"What would you like?"

"Twinkle, twinkle, little star?"

He sighed, then went to fetch his keyboard, and had to whistle because Gus greeted him with trilling notes. He closed both doors, bedroom and hall, and brought the keyboard to the dining table. He told her, "You can wear the head phones."

"That's unnerving. Why won't you listen?"

"There are times, Roberta, when you have to trust— when you throw your hat over the windmill and *live*. This is one of those times."

"Wow. I'm glad you warned me, and I didn't experience it unknowingly."

He played brilliantly. He did the "Five Finger Exercise" perfectly. It was so unexpectedly lovely that her eyes teared. And he smiled. She begged for another piece, but he said he'd promised only one.

He looked at her seriously. "You need to know that I keep my promises. I'll play for you another time. Your choices. Is that good enough?"

"You led me so cleverly into believing you couldn't play. Are you a devious man?"

"When it counts," he agreed.

"What does that mean?"

"You can trust me never to harm you."

She frowned. "Is that the answer?"

"I'll elaborate, if it's necessary."

"You didn't say you wouldn't trick me, only that you wouldn't harm me."

He watched her. Then he smiled. "Are you going to choose one of the matchsticks?"

"I shall choose my own team."

"You are irritatingly unleadable."

"That's strange, my father always says that."

"What does your mother say about you?"

"She calls me 'Tate-Fred-George, uh, *Bob*! Hillary has it the worst of all, being youngest. And it's annoying, waiting until mother stops, so we know who she wants. Tate has an expectant look all the time, since mother always starts with her name."

"I didn't ask what she calls you, but what she says about you. How does she label you?"

"Precious."

"As contrary as you are, and she says you're *precious*? How does she figure that?"

"She calls us 'precious' since she can't remember our names and gets tired of going down the list."

"Well, that does explain the labeling." He grinned, inviting her to be sassy.

But she passed on the chance that time. "Let's go out and walk. When does the game begin?"

"We have time."

As they walked the four miles, easily and pleasantly, he pretended to be afraid of her cast, which she swung easily, since it was lighter than the first one. She told him he had nothing to fear from her since he wasn't a masher. He wondered how she couldn't know?

The Super Bowl viewed with Roberta was almost a man's dream of a day. She was wearing a yellow velvet lounge suit that caressed her body the way he longed to do. Her hair was a black cloud around her head, her blue eyes were alert and animated, and she entered completely into the spirit of the game.

She didn't choose her team until after the first quarter. Graham's team started out with a bang, getting a touchdown and field goal, and everybody knows that in a Super Bowl, the team that scores first will win. He even told that to Roberta and advised her to save her twenty cents, but she chose the underdog.

He would have thought any smart women with two brain cells would have sided with him. He scowled at her. She was gorgeous, and it didn't matter one bit whether or not she liked the team he liked. If she asked him, he'd change sides and root for her team. He'd argue for a while first, but he'd change sides eventually.

But why would she choose the underdog? Well, he thought, what would you expect from an environmentalist? This whole world was the underdog, and she was trying to save it. Why not a football team on a Sunday afternoon?

He had to leave Sunday night to go back to Georgia. He offered Roberta the use of his car, but she declined. "I would miss all the regulars on the bus route. They'd worry about me. And I don't have a place to park. Parking in D.C. is impossible."

He took some of her books from her shelves and along with the advice books, put them into a briefcase. He cleaned Gus's cage and put ample food and water in the bowls. He whispered, "Be quiet. Hum, don't sing. Got that? If she finds you and I'm not here to protect her, it's over two hundred and fifty bucks shot to hell. You do understand?"

The mouse hummed.

A mouse couldn't possibly understand English in just a week, could it? Dogs did. But mice?

He closed his doors carefully and said, "Well..." He wondered if Roberta would give up a goodbye kiss. She didn't come close or reach or lick her lips. She smiled and said, "I'm sorry your team lost. You owe me twenty cents."

"What twenty cents? Have you a note? Did you tape the conversation? Gambling is illegal. I can't be a part of anything illegal."

She gasped indignantly, and he smiled beatifically. He said, "Don't cry your eyes out. I'll be back Tuesday."

"Goodbye."

"You may use my TV."

"I'd planned to."

"You're *supposed* to ask permission. Didn't your mother ever tell you that?"

"May I use your TV while you're gone?"

"Yes, you may."

"See? So why did I have to ask? I knew you wouldn't mind," she pointed out.

"It's the principle of the thing."

"Oh,"

"Miss me."

"I shall—"

His lips parted and he drew in a thrilled, silent breath.

"—be thinking of a way to get that twenty cents you owe me."

He didn't read anything but what he had to for the deposition. He daydreamed of ways she could get the twenty-cent bet out of him or get him to tell state secrets or learn how he got the scar on his backside. Sex. Anything she wanted.

When he eagerly returned on Tuesday, it was to an empty apartment. There was no note. She'd known he was coming home that day. What amount of time would it have taken to write "Hello" on a sheet of paper? She could have done that without any trouble at all.

He might have known she wouldn't be there. Just because he had missed her like a fool and hoped she'd be there, didn't mean she would be.

Gus was fine. His pellet bowl had hardly been touched, his cage was still quite clean, with plenty of water. He trilled a welcome.

Graham asked, "How'd it go?"

Gus trilled several different notes.

Graham frowned at the mouse. "Are you trying to communicate? Listen, mouse, don't get friendly. You are here for one purpose and that purpose only. You're to scare the beejeebers out of Roberta on cue. Got that? And that's all."

The mouse was standing up on its hind legs and watching. Graham snubbed the creature and emptied his suitcase, separating his clothes into the laundry basket, drawers and the closet. When everything was tidy, he lifted the cage up onto the desk so the mouse could look out the window.

Graham ignored the pleased sounds Gus was making, and stomped off to the living room, carefully shutting both his doors on the exuberant trilling.

He finally remembered that this was the week that the agency's environmental report was to be mailed. They needed volunteers.

Still in his suit, he went out and caught the bus.

Roberta was astonished to see him, and a little distracted. She took him at his word and led him to a room where there were several stacks of paper on tables. People were walking along, picking up a sheet from each pile, and gathering them into a sheaf, which they handed to a person at the end of the table. There the sheaf was stapled and put in another pile. Simple work. Needed.

He began, and Roberta vanished.

He worked four hours. Starving, he went in search of Roberta only to find that she had left to go to a fund-raiser in order to see a senator and say two words to him. Tired, disappointed, raising his hands to ward off the others' thanks for his time, he left.

He took the bus home, and she wasn't there, either. He made a sandwich and drank a beer. Then he showered, put on pajamas and went into the living room to watch the news. He went soundly to sleep.

He wakened in the morning on the sofa with a blanket over him and a pillow under his head. He looked at his watch. He found it was two minutes before he usually got up. Waking up at the regular time gave him satisfaction and the feeling of being in control. Even a dog can do that, or salivate at the sound of a dinner bell.

He took some comfort that she'd covered him. What did she think, seeing him there? Had she stood and filled her eyes with him, as he wished to do with her? Had she been tempted to lay her hands on him, as he longed to do to her?

Or had she simply thought him a fool for not going to bed?

No note in the kitchen. No welcome home or thanks for helping out at her office. Nothing. Had he only helped that fine agency in order to impress Roberta and win Brownie points? Yes.

He made the coffee for them both as now was his habit. He had cereal and milk. He left, having carefully closed both his doors. And he delivered the deposition to the attorney who hadn't had the time to go to Georgia.

Then he asked for two days off to take care of personal business. His superior said an absentminded "Sure. Go ahead."

He went back to Roberta's office, and he worked all that day. The permanent people were charmed by him, the volunteers amazed. He was in a suit and tie, but he discarded the jacket and tie and rolled up his sleeves. His blond hair was mussed, his face earnest, and he was quick.

Roberta shared her sack lunch, so he had a half sandwich, a half apple and half of a caramel. He said to her, "That's not enough food."

And she said, "I'm fine. That's all I generally eat."

He looked at her blankly, then remembered she was from a family of girls and probably didn't realize men had appetites she'd never dreamed about. Yes. That was true. All sorts of appetites. And his needed her.

He found a gofer, sent out for five pizzas and shared them among the volunteers. They were pleased; he was hungry. Roberta was doing something else.

He went back the next day, too. She asked, "Why are you doing this?"

Why couldn't she figure it out? He replied with only a touch of irony, "We have no other planet."

She nodded thoughtfully.

When her day was over, they rode the bus home together, and with their eyes on Graham her public transportation cohorts said sly hellos to her.

She had the next three nights scheduled. Tonight was Gus's Big Night.

Five

———

They separated in the living room to change clothes. Graham went into his segment of the apartment and quickly closed the door. He was already whistling, since Gus now tended to greet him so vocally. He went into the bedroom and leaned over the cage on the desk. "Brace yourself, buddy, this is your Big Night! I'll change first, so get yourself psyched up. You have about five minutes."

Graham used the electric razor to take off the worst of his beard, then rinsed off in the shower. He pulled on clean clothes and smoothed on only a whisper of after-shave. He smiled at his image and mouthed: "Good luck."

He picked up the cage and carried it to his door. He pep-whispered the entire way. "Go boldly and give a trill to attract her attention, and that will do it. No bit-ing. Got that? I'll be there right away, right after the scream. Okay, team, let's hit it.''

He bent down and opened the cage door, and the mouse looked around, fascinated by the new territory. He stayed put.

With glances toward the kitchen where Roberta was clanking pans and running water and so on, Graham tilted the cage and shook it a little, but that only spilled some of the water and made the pellets slide off onto the carpet.

Graham leaned close and hissed through his teeth, ''Git!'' And he joggled the cage.

Gus went out into the big world and looked around, amazed. Intimidated? Graham was disgusted. He reached out a toe and nudged the mouse in the right direction. But Gus darted aside and disappeared under the sofa.

Graham was shocked. A two-hundred-fifty-dollar mouse. They should have rehearsed. He put the cage down in his hall and went grimly into the living room and looked around. The damned mouse could be anywhere by then. He searched stealthily, getting down and looking under the sofa.

''Lose something?''

He jerked up guiltily and smiled. ''Uh...a... button.''

''I have a button box. Maybe I can match it.''

She stood there. Unsuspecting. Vulnerable. Where the hell was Gus? Graham sent his gaze around but there was no mouse anywhere in sight.

He said lamely, ''It probably went back into the bedroom.'' He got up, went to his open door and glanced back. She was watching him with an odd expression on her face, and he realized just what he'd said. So he added, "The button rolled back."

He vanished, and she returned to the kitchen. There in the middle of it was a *mouse*, sitting up, and it *trilled* at her. Instead of a hoarse squeak, she screamed a full-throated, marvelous clarion sound, and she grabbed the broom.

Graham was looking under his bed when Roberta shrieked, and then he knew that Gus was where he was supposed to be; in the kitchen.

Graham smiled. He stood slowly and moved to the rescue when he heard a broom go *whap, whap, whap!*

And Roberta yelled, "I got him! I got him, *left-handed*!"

She'd killed Gus.

Never in all his fantasizing had *Gus* figured in anything after Roberta's scream. Now Gus was dead.

Graham ran to the kitchen and Roberta flung herself into his arms, right on schedule. He stood there where he wanted to be, and looked down in horror at the tiny figure lying still on the floor. The enormous, lethal, biodegradable broom was there beside the broken little body.

From the shelter of Graham's loose embrace, Roberta looked back at the body and said in some surprise, "It's really quite small."

Tiny little Gus, the two-hundred-fifty-dollar mouse.

Roberta was somewhat stimulated. She had her arms wrapped around Graham's neck and she was saying, "I killed it! I was very brave."

He moved his hands on her back in a motion that he needed. It was a comforting. He said, "I'll bury it."

Roberta clutched Graham. She shrieked, "It *moved*!"

Gus was alive? In a brilliant flash of inspiration, Graham croaked, "Rigor mortis." His hard arms enclosed Roberta and his body sighed in ecstasy, but his distracted brain make his big hand jam her face into his shoulder so she couldn't see that Gus was alive.

How to save the mouse? Graham said to Roberta, "I'll take care of this. Go on into the living room. This'll be a little messy."

She quite willingly left the kitchen, while Graham bent over Gus. Gus opened his eyes, gave a quick look around and trilled! So Graham had to whistle—what? for God's sake—and he turned it into the funeral dirge. It sounded shockingly like gallows humor. But the damned mouse was telling him about the monster in the kitchen. Graham scooped the complaining mouse into his hand, and still whistling, he went to the coat closet.

Roberta asked, "What are you doing?"

His face blank, Graham looked at his curiosity-ridden, murderous love. "It's biodegradable. I thought I'd bury it."

"I haven't buried a pet in fifteen years. We need a matchbox." She went busily into the kitchen.

"We?" She was going to help? Now, how was he going to avoid burying a live mouse? He put Gus's body up his jacket sleeve and buttoned the cuff. Then he held his two hands together, cupped.

Roberta returned with the box, saying, "The matches are wrapped in aluminum foil on the first shelf. Here."

He took the box and walked toward the front door, moving his hands to open and close the box. As he went out the door, he said, "I've a snow shovel in my car. I'll get that."

He walked to the corner of the building, then ran to his car. He had a spare key under the back bumper. He opened the trunk, took a square rag, put Gus in it and securely tied the four corners together. Gus could breathe, but he couldn't get out.

But he might.

So Graham put the rag into his toolbox. He'd be back as soon as he could. He carried the shovel and the empty matchbox back to the stream. Roberta was outside in her jacket, waiting.

Being the housekeeper she was, she'd seen the pellets by Graham's door. Curious, she'd opened the door and seen the cage. The mouse was a pet? Why hadn't he mentioned it? She looked at Graham rather oddly and proffered some ivy she had gathered for the grave. He thought she was very sweet when he considered she'd only seen Gus just that one, emotionally upsetting time.

With the blunt snow shovel, he turned the first root-resistent opening for the grave. "Does it have to be six feet down?"

She replied, "No."

Graham gave her a glance and noted that she was still filled with adrenaline from her encounter. This was exactly what he'd anticipated. Now he had to save the damned mouse. She had really whapped it. Well, she hadn't known the mouse, so why should she have hesitated? Mice weren't on the endangered list. Very few women would be concerned if they were.

The empty box was buried, the ivy planted on the grave, and they returned to the apartment. She stopped in the middle of the living room and stood before him to smile up at him. "You're really very sweet."

Now was the time. He opened his arms, and she came to him. He hugged her tightly against his willing body, and he groaned in an agony of need and desire. But there was that mouse out there in his toolbox, injured, slowly being asphyxiated.

Graham kissed Roberta with great passion, his hands hard and moving.... Then he set her away from him. In a voice that was roughened and just a little harsh, he said, "I have an appointment. I'll be back later."

That surprised Roberta a little. She didn't reply but just stared at him.

He turned his head to the side and kissed her again. And he did hesitate, because he needed to get the cage from his room. "I need some things." He backed away awkwardly and went into his room, closing the door. He put the cage into a laundry sack and put some things around it. Then he gathered up the two how-to books, and again closing his doors, walked back to the living room. He saw that Roberta still stood in the middle of the room.

"I'll be back." He dropped both handsful of junk and pulled her against him hungrily to kiss her feverishly. But again he set her aside. And for the third time, he said, "I'll be back."

He took a deep breath and left the apartment. He got Gus out of the rag and laid the little body in the cage. He turned on the car's heater and hurriedly drove to the veterinarian's. He went inside and told Sheila, "It's an emergency."

She took him to a tiny cubbyhole, and pretty soon the vet appeared. "What's the matter?"

"She hit him with a broom."

The vet didn't smile. As she examined Gus, the
mouse told her all about it. Then she put the creature
back into his cage, and he took tentative steps.

Graham was astonished.

The vet leaned against the examining table and
folded her arms over her nice chest. "I would like to
know you better. Are you involved?"

Graham looked at the woman seriously. He sighed
regretfully and nodded. "With a woman who doesn't
understand mice."

"Your ploy worked, but you left her to get help for
the mouse."

"We buried an empty box."

She moved to the door. "I'll find a home for the
mouse. Singing ones are quite charming. People like
them—in cages." She gave him a look before she
added, "If it doesn't work out with her, come by and
see him. Gus, isn't it?"

"If it doesn't work out with Roberta, I've planned
to become a Presbyterian monk."

She nodded in understanding. "Well, if being a
Presbyterian monk isn't the answer, I'll still be here."

"You've been very kind to me. Thank you."

By then, Gus was sitting up and cleaning his whiskers. Graham and the vet watched him. Gus then ran
around his cage and saw there were some pellets left.
He settled down, nibbling. Graham said, "I thought
only cats had nine lives."

The vet chuckled low in her throat and looked up at
the man. She said, "I really hope it works out for you.
But does she deserve you?"

"It's the other way around." Graham was sure.

So he got back to the apartment, empty-handed, and
there was a note. Roberta had written, "They called

from the office. The last of the mailings have to be sent out tonight. Thanks for taking care of the mouse. Roberta."

She'd contrived that to avoid being with him. He'd rushed her. He needed to back off. Maybe not. He'd see how she acted when he saw her again. He'd wait up.

He vacuumed up the food pellets he'd spilled in his doorway. Then he took the sack of pellets and the water out to his car and put them in the trunk. He'd return them to the vet the next day. He began to go over the men he knew who would appreciate a woman like the vet. There were a couple.

He waited until midnight, then he went to bed. She was avoiding him. Friday morning he got up, and she was cleaning. she said, "Oh, good, I need to vacuum. I didn't want to start the machine while you slept."

That irritated him. The first time she'd seen him since he'd saved her from Gus and she said she needed to vacuum. There's a lover's greeting for you.

She said, "Something dug up the mouse and left the empty box."

"Yeah?"

"Who would dig up a dead mouse?"

"Grave robbers? Maybe from a med school? For organ transplants?"

She watched him with great patience, in a very waiting way.

He explained, "The world is full of strange happenings." He filled a glass with orange juice.

"Don't you find it unsettling that I screamed bloody murder...and no one heard me? A woman is always secure in the knowledge that, if she screams, someone will come charging to the rescue."

"I heard, but you didn't need me."

"You were very brave to pick it up with your bare hand."

"It couldn't hurt me." He sipped the juice. "Did you get the mailings finished?"

"Yes. We worked until almost two."

"Why did it have to be done...that day?"

"Scheduling. We need to inform our contributors so that they will know what we're up against. Then when we ask for contributions, they know why."

He nodded. She was wearing one of those insidiously maddening velvet lounge suits over her bare and luscious body. It was orange. She looked like sherbet—nicely formed sherbet. He said, "I know you're scheduled to go to something today. I'll clean when I get home, or tomorrow. I have nothing else to do."

"I was wondering. If you *really* have nothing to do, if you'd...maybe...like to go along? I was given another ticket."

He perked up.

"It's a cocktail-buffet, and it will be elegant. Then there's a public reception with cheeses and wine. We could spend the evening eating and drinking. Can you hold your liquor?"

"I don't drink much. Why did you ask me?"

"If you'd rather not..." She let it hang.

"No, I'd enjoy it. But there must be others you should ask."

"The extra ticket was a surprise. One of our contributors sent it to the office. There isn't anyone I know who needs to be there, so I'm free to ask someone I want to take along."

He smiled.

She wasn't looking at him, and she added, "And at this particular one, I dread having to cope with one man who will be there." She named the man. "We call him Joe Blow. I have to be courteous, but he... touches. I hate it."

She wanted him for protection, not from a mouse but from a rat. He could do that. How much of that did she have to endure? His jealousy rose in him and he said, "I would be delighted. Give me a list of who can touch and who can't."

She gave him a rather strange look and replied, "He's the only one who is aggressively insulting."

"The others are okay?"

"The others keep their hands to themselves." She frowned at him. "Are you implying that I allow some gropers to indulge in tickle-and-slap for the good of the environment?"

"No. I just wanted to know if you would only need my attention sporadically."

"You don't need to come along, at all."

"I'm anticipating it." He smiled at her. "Thank you for the invitation."

But she had her back up, and she replied coolly, "You're welcome. Blue suit, white shirt, red tie."

"I have three sets of each."

"Good."

"Any man in government has such a uniform. Two at the least. One at the cleaners and one ready to go."

"Fine."

"And dark shoes."

"Fine."

"And linen handkerchiefs."

She turned and gave him another rather impatient look. He smiled. She asked, "Are you being asinine?"

"No."

"Good."

"What time?"

She looked at her watch. "Meet me at the Senate Office Building at six on the dot."

"Check."

And she finally grinned.

They met in the arriving crowd and Roberta thought he looked gorgeous. He smiled at her and his gaze went over her in a very masculine way. But with this man, she liked it. They went to the hearing room where the catered affair was scheduled. They milled in the crush of people who packed in just for the opportunity to clutch an elbow—however briefly—to be seen, and maybe to be in some picture for the paper back home. There was always the scrapbook.

He suggested, "Tell me specifically who you want to see. I'm great at working crowds. You've put yourself in the right hands."

"Just keep me out of Joe's."

With great ease and no stepped-on toes, Graham managed to get her next to and speaking with the people she needed to see. It amazed Roberta. Graham was so courteous, so big, and he could maneuver beautifully. When she commented on it, he replied it was a lot like carrying a football downfield. When they met Joe, he was enthusiastic about seeing Roberta. He reached for her but his hands ran into Graham.

Roberta laughed in delight, and Joe thought she laughed for his benefit and was glad to see him. He reached again, and once more his hands ran into Graham. It was uncanny. Without being touched once, Roberta got in her pitch for a particular bit of legislation. And she was impressed. She hugged Graham's arm to her chest, and he was briefly immobilized. She didn't mind being touched by him. Or maybe she didn't realize what she was doing.

They had a good time. Roberta said, "This is fun! I never had such a good time. You have been fabulous. I'm so glad you came."

Another lobbyist purred, "Are you an environmentalist?" as she took Graham's arm and maneuvered between him and Roberta.

Graham asked Roberta, "Is she on the list?"

Roberta replied, "She's just a lobbyist."

Graham told the woman, "I'm a waste of your time."

She said, "I doubt that."

Roberta told her, "I saw him first."

And the woman said, "Hell," and let go of Graham. But her hand lingered on his, and after the suggestive tickle, she curled his hand around her business card.

He tucked the card carefully into Roberta's décolletage, and she laughed up at him.

He told her, "This is fun."

She agreed. "Today has been. You have made it a treat. But it's really work. These affairs aren't free. They are used to raise money for politicians. So we pay to come here. It's a contact we can't afford to miss.

"When I was first here, I was a wide-eyed innocent. I didn't even know who I was supposed to contact. The lobbyists and politicians see each other all the time, and over the years, they've created a camaraderie that is exclusive. It's hard to break in and get time. I stood around a lot. It's like being a new congressman."

He understood. "It's that way in every profession. A practicing lawyer has all the mistakes to make. If he's lucky, he comes under the mentorship of an old hand. Jim..." But he didn't want to talk to Roberta about Jim.

She nodded. "Jim... That was McFarland, wasn't it? Was he your mentor?"

Tersely, Graham said, "Yes." As always, he gave credit. "He saved my neck more than once. He taught me to anticipate disaster and figure how to handle it. It's really part of problem solving; it's just learning how the law can be applied."

"We find that's true in environmental law. I would like to meet Jim. He sounds like a good friend."

Graham had no reply to that.

Roberta had seen those whom she'd come to see, and it had been so easy, with Graham there to run interference for her. She told him, "You tend to negate your football expertise, but you do such a good job getting me through the crush, you must have been magnificent."

"I played football all those years just to help you out today. I put my fragile body on the line because I knew there would come a day when Roberta Lambert would need me."

"And you buried the mouse."

He thought of the last time he'd seen Gus, singing in the vet's office. Graham smiled at Roberta and said, "Like football games, life takes strange turns, doesn't it?"

"I'm glad you answered my ad for an apartment-mate."

His mind deleted the word "apartment" from her sentence.

She was close to him in the crowd, and she was smiling up at him and teasing. She was soft, and she didn't appear to notice all the times she was pressed against him. He noticed.

They ate their share of the goodies, and she said, "For me, this is supper. But there are those who will meet at a dinner later on. Lobbyists generally don't eat much, because we all go to several parties, and if we ate at each party, we would get fat. The leftovers are given to the Second Harvest people, who then feed the hungry. So the hungry are fed by people who are afraid of getting fat. That's a strange thing, isn't it?"

They took a cab to their next appointment. While Graham paid the fare, he saw that Roberta paid his way into the party. She did it with such courteous discretion that, if he hadn't been keenly aware of her and exactly what she was doing, he wouldn't have known. She had the extra ticket only to the first affair. The admission into this one was expensive.

Her wanting him with her charmed him. She could have told him from the beginning that she was inviting him just to the first gathering. She could have sold him a ticket. She could have done a number of things, but she was so discreet in paying his way to the second party, that he allowed it.

But he was very tender with her. He saw to it that she had ample time with each of the contacts she needed. As big as he was and as kind as he seemed, he managed to keep everyone at bay until she took a step back. He'd noticed that was an unconscious indication she was finished.

She did a good job of lobbying. She was earnest and concise. She asked only for consideration. The people she spoke to listened to everyone who approached them, but it seemed to Graham that she was the most businesslike while still courteous, with that extra, inbred graciousness of a lady. He was proud of her.

They took the Metro home. They were pleasantly tired and needed no more food. They changed, and Graham's earnest offer to help her out of her clothes was laughingly rejected. He went into his room and looked automatically at the empty corner for Gus. He missed a mouse?

He put on old white jeans that were soft and comfortable. And his T-shirt was brown like his eyes. He smiled into the mirror and slipped one of the foil packets into his back pocket.

She was in the kitchen when he walked in. Her hair was down around her shoulders in a lovely silken swirl, and she was wearing a red velvet lounge suit that about set him on his ear. Again she had on nothing under it and it caressed her body lovingly. He couldn't breathe. He moved as if the atmosphere had become leaden, and it was difficult for him to get across the room.

She asked, "Are you at all hungry?"

She was talking about food. "What do you have?"

She turned from the sink and scoffed. "After all the food you've had this afternoon, you can't possibly be serious. That was just one of those questions that start a conversation."

She wanted to talk to him? "Asking what you have to eat is a way of carrying on the conversation. Who knows? You might have made some Rice Krispie-marshmallow treat, for all I know."

"You're really hooked on that?"

"Everybody has a weak spot."

"Is that the only one you have? Any other quirks?"

He went closer to her and touched his chest and his hip and thigh against her body. "I like women in red velvet. It drives me crazy."

Was she appalled? No, she laughed, as if that was exactly why she wore it. So he curled his hand around the nape of her neck, and his other hand tilted up her face to his so that he could look at her. "You're wearing red velvet."

Her eyes were enormous, and her lips moved with difficulty. "Well, I'll be darned."

"Do you know what happens to women who wear red velvet?" His big hand had slid from her nape down her back, where his fingers spread to pull her body closer to his tingling excitement. His other hand went around her head to brace it, and his fingers tangled in the black, silken tresses.

With his hot, sweet breath on her cheek, she asked slowly, "What happens to women who wear red velvet?"

And he kissed her. It was remarkable. Since it wasn't a surprise that he was going to kiss her, how could it be so astonishing? It was a puzzle he'd have to work on another time, because now his brain was swamped with sensation and was not functioning.

He lifted his mouth to allow his lungs to gasp in air, and he was trembling. Everything in him was excited. His body, his hands, his breath. He tried to relax, but his gaze was glued to her, and he licked his lips.

He was embarrassed that he had so little control, but then he saw her head wobble. And his eyes glinted fires as he realized he hadn't been the only one surprised by that flammable kiss. He ran his hand up and then down

a bit lower on her back in a caressing motion, and he
found no resistance when he pulled her head against his
chest and lay his cheek on top of her head.

They stood like that for a while, recovering from one
kiss. One kiss. He'd anticipated just such a kiss. Those
she'd given him after she thought she'd killed Gus
didn't really count because he'd been distracted. This
one counted. This was their first kiss. This was how it
should be. Except that he ought to have more control.

In a croaking voice, he said, "My God, woman,
you're ruining me."

She turned up her glazed eyes and frowned a little.
"I'm ruining you? What do you think you're doing to
me?"

His voice wouldn't work on the first two tries but he
finally asked, speaking up over the loud wheezing of
his breath, "What...am I...doing to you?"

She moved back and earnestly replied, "I'm not
sure. My equilibrium seems haywire." She gestured
languidly. "My lungs are having trouble, and I feel
funny."

"Where? Where do you feel funny?" He seemed
concerned.

"Maybe I had too much to drink?"

"No. I watched. I wanted you sober."

"You wanted me sober?" She frowned at him.
"Why?"

"So you wouldn't get me mixed up with anybody
else who's made love to you."

Six

———

"Are you going to make love to me?" Roberta looked up at Graham very seriously.

"You're wearing red velvet."

She looked down at her excited bosom and said, "I suppose it wouldn't save me to take off the red velvet?"

His tongue tangled as he hastened to say, "It would be a last-ditch effort, but you could try."

She stepped back and put her hand on the bottom of her sweatshirt. She looked at him. "I'll be right back."

"Wait! No! You have to do it here."

"In the kitchen?"

"I have to see if taking it off will save you."

"Ohhh."

"Let me help. Your cast. Hey, you won't bloody my nose, will you?"

"You're a masher of a different sort. Your nose is safe."

He helped her out of her top, maneuvering her into the living room. Then he had to step back and look at her. "You're beautiful." His words were somewhat fuzzy.

"I'm just average." She was uncertain.

"You're a gorgeous average."

She confessed, "The rest of me is just like everyone else."

"Your bottom half isn't at all like mine."

Her gaze quickly dropped down him and she nodded. "You're right." She smiled, just a little.

He cleared his throat. "Let me see the rest."

"I've never done this before." She gestured vaguely. "And I'm not sure this isn't too quickly done."

"This first time can't be quick enough for— First time?" he asked carefully.

"I just haven't ever gotten around to sex."

He stared in shock. A virgin. How had she escaped? And he would initiate her. He licked his lips and practiced breathing in and out. "Honey, let's put your shirt back on for a while. We need to go slower."

"You don't want to." She was disappointed.

He laughed and sputtered before he finally managed to say, "Yes, I most certainly do."

"You're not laughing at me?" she asked, looking vulnerable.

He whispered, "Oh, Roberta!" and enclosed her in such a cherishing hug that she couldn't misunderstand. "I want this to be nice for you. I just want to go slower."

"But you will?" She helped one-handedly to pull the top back over her head and settle it in place.

"Only fire or flood—"

"Check the stream."

Again she'd surprised him. His eyes sparkled, and the flames in him leaped high. This was going to be delicious agony.

Very seriously, she asked, "What do I do? How do we begin?"

"Do what you want to."

"I need to sit down, my legs are wobbly."

He led her to the sofa and helped her sit down. Then he sat next to her, as he expressed rather intense interest. "What do you suppose causes wobbly knees?"

"It's very strange."

He put his arms around her and pulled her sweet, soft body close to his desperate one. Then he kissed her again. Lightning went through him, burning and searing, probably short-circuiting his brain. He kissed her again. And he couldn't estimate the damage because his thinking was fuzzy and only on one track. He asked her, "How are the knees?"

"There are other problems." She had a hard time forming the words. Her head was back, her body lax and malleable, her arms up, her hand and cast helpless at the back of his head.

He laid his hot hand on her knee. "Not here?"

"I can't tell. But my stomach is rioting."

He lifted his head. "You're . . . nauseated?"

She struggled to laugh. Her eyes were closed as if she was coming out of a swoon. "It's as if a big tongue leisurely lapped up my stomach . . . inside."

He put a trembly hand on her stomach and pressed a hard swirl in the red velvet. "There?"

She purred, "Umm." Her puffy lips smiled, and her eyes blinked lazily.

"You like that? Having your tummy rubbed?"

She did only a fair job of nodding, and the smile stayed. But her body moved in a tiny sinuous way, and she made that sound in her throat again.

His hair stood on end, all over, and he began to sweat. He licked his lips, then nuzzled her throat and paid attention to her ear, with his tongue exploring and his lips nipping and his breath giving her goose bumps. He kissed her receptive mouth again, and this time she arched her body into his, and her hand and wrists pulled on his shoulders. And it was he who smiled.

He kissed her cheek and around under her chin to see if the other ear was as sensitive. And it was. She moved against him in the onslaught of thrills, as his hand swirled around her stomach and up over her breasts, making her gasp. He lifted his head. "Like that?" And his hand kneaded to show her what he was talking about.

She made a throaty sound that was half exclamation, half chuckle.

And he labored to say, "Me, too."

It wasn't long before his swirling hand had abandoned the red velvet to slide under her top. There he explored her silken skin to find the satin nipple and used his finger and thumb to tug it into a peak.

He released her to pull off his T-shirt and toss it aside. His eyes were fiery and intent on her, his breath high in his chest. His body was hot and steamy. He lifted her top off and dropped it to the floor. Then he very carefully lifted her body against his and slowly rubbed his heated, hairy chest against her sensitive breasts.

She moaned and her head rolled back, exposing her throat so his scalding mouth could suck and lick along the tender flesh. With some effort, she managed to lift her hand to his head, and she used her wrists to pull him to her. Her mouth—opened, hungry, astonishing in its passion—sought his.

He shuddered, holding her tightly to him, holding her still. Then he had to release her and stand up, to turn away, to breathe, to lean over and brace his hands on his knees as he fought for control.

Lying back, abandoned on the sofa, she watched, still and fascinated, as he straightened and rubbed his chest and walked to the window to look outside. Then he stood and just breathed for a while, still rubbing his chest, and he finally turned back to her. His voice was husky. "You sure try a man's limits."

She wasn't exactly sure what he meant.

He came to her. "I would very much like for this to be slow and easy, but I'm not sure I can handle you. You drive me right up the wall."

She'd never seen a man in passion. He was filmed with sweat. His hair was tumbled, and it trembled. He was so tensed that tiny, almost invisible tremors beset him. She because concerned for him and reached her hand to the side of his face. He turned his mouth and kissed her palm, then he said, "I'll sure try, but honey, just know there's a limit."

She slowly stated the fact. "You need to make love to me."

"Badly."

"All right." Softly she gave permission.

He gathered her back to him and groaned with his desire. "It'll be so fast you might not even notice."

She laughed low in her throat. "I think I would."

He stood up and gave her his hand to help her stand.

She wobbled. "The knee problem." She looked up at him as she explained.

He had to hug her for that. Then he lifted her. She was amazed. Right then, he could have picked up the entire apartment complex. He carried her into his room and was careful of her head and feet as he took her through the doorways. Then he lay her on his bed, telling her, "It's time you got here in person." And he was out of his jeans in no time and picked them back up to find the packet. He put that on, which was remarkable, with his body and his hands trembling as they were. And he came down on the bed beside her.

They got her out of the rest of her clothes, and he had to admire her. His hands had to touch, his eyes to study and his mouth to taste.

Although he was mesmerized with passion, she was somewhat hesitant. "Will it fit?"

And he knew she was uncertain. "Easily. You were made for me."

She whispered, "I suppose it must."

"Don't be afraid."

"Let's try it."

He touched her. "You may not believe this, but you are ready for me."

"Okay." She lay flat, looking at the ceiling. She licked her lips and said, "Do it."

He wondered if there'd ever been a man, especially a loving man, who had been so thrilled by a woman's gift of herself. How could he be quick with her now? He put his hand on her stomach. "Does my hand feel different on your stomach?" He was distracting her.

She nodded minutely and looked at him. "Bold."

"If you think that's bold, what about this?" And he ran fingers down into her maiden hair and tugged gently.

"Scandalous." She sighed.

Easing a finger down to her wet heat, he asked, "What about that?" Her thighs had tensed.

"Outrageous." She said the word in a gasp.

He leaned his mouth to her breast and kissed under it, pushing it up with his face, nuzzling. "And that?"

She managed to tell him, "That affects the inside of my stomach again."

Rubbing his face into the side of her throat, he licked into her ear, making her squeal. "And that?"

"A very strange type of goose bumps, inside my stomach."

Then he bent over her, with his hand in her maiden hair, and he suckled her nipple. He did it leisurely, pulling it into his mouth, his tongue stroking under it, pressing it to the roof of his mouth, his teeth barely grazing the tender flesh. And his hard hand moved, his fingers reached, and one long finger stroked her fires.

He didn't have to ask, then. She moved and pressed up. She became very frustrated and made sounds and movements of need. He lifted his head and smiled at her. Then he raised himself over her and eased down on her as she welcomed him. And it was her hand that placed him. He pressed in hesitantly but her hands grabbed the small of his back, her cast banging him, and he laughed as he sank into her heat.

He shivered with passion fires so concentrated his breath was scorching. He hesitated, fighting for time, and then he moved.

Her body went wild in trying to consume all of him. She needed more, and she knew that, but she wasn't sure what to do. She squirmed and gasped and struggled until they floundered to the peak, very disorganized and amazed, and hit that ultimate pause before the crashing tumult of release. They lay back to float, to shimmer with the aftershocks, which lessened like faraway echoes, to lie contented, released, spent.

He was immobilized. He lay inert. She was stimulated. She laughed throatily. She held him against her with her casted hand and used her free hand to pet him. She murmured, "Marvelous" and "Umm" and "Ahhh."

"Delilah." His word was smothered because his face was buried beside hers in the bed, on her hair, with his mouth against her neck.

She corrected him gently, "Roberta."

"Delilah. She ruined Samson just like you've ruined me."

Lazily she instructed, "She cut his hair. That's what did it."

"That's the censored version," he murmured.

Very softly, she said, "That was wonderful."

"You are. You saved my life."

She picked up his limp hand and dropped it. "Apparently it was a completed job. You're not very lively."

"You drained me. As soon as my juices replenish, I'll be fine."

"Uh, about these…juices. As I understand it, you're in this shape because you had too much, and you are now depleted and ruined. So if your juices are replenished, wouldn't that mean you'd have to go through this whole process again and be ruined again?"

"No one ever said a man's lot was easy."

She laughed and hugged him.

He dragged up and slowly, carefully separated from her. Then he said, "Don't move," and he went into the bathroom. She pulled the coverlet over her and waited.

He returned and climbed into bed with her, taking her back into his arms. He asked. "Do you know how many times I've fantasized about you in these last thirty years?"

"You're thirty?"

"Thirty-one. I was a late bloomer and didn't begin thinking about making love until I was a year old. It's been my main thought almost constantly since then." He kissed her. "How long have you fantasized about me?"

"I never did."

"You must have. My telepathic thoughts must have communicated with yours."

"I've been curious. Have you had a great many women? You are good."

"I suppose it's not manly to say I have so little experience. But I haven't."

"I'm glad you had protection for me."

He kissed her again. "You feel so nice against my bare skin. Adam must have been so glad to get Eve."

"Where was your farm in Indiana?"

"Near Fort Wayne."

"I don't know much about Indiana."

"It's the garden spot of the world. It's the home of the Indianapolis Colts and the Hoosier Dome. And Indiana University is in Bloomington. Where they filmed *Breaking Away*, a brilliant film about the Little 500, which is a bike race."

"My. All that?"

"And me."

"Lucky Indiana."

"They don't realize that yet. But they will probably dig up my body in a hundred years or so, and carry it back to Indiana to be interred in a glorious—but not ostentatious—monument on the Circle in Indianapolis."

"Not at Fort Wayne?"

"There'll be a long legal battle over where they'll put my bones, but Indianapolis will win."

"Why will they do this?"

"Well, I don't actually know yet. But then I never believed I'd find you."

She laughed, amused by him.

Huskily he told her, "You jiggle when you laugh." And his hands cupped her.

"Your juices can't be replenished this soon."

"I believe it's true. Let's test it." He gave her a lovely, squishy kiss, and she felt him stir. He exclaimed. "You've saved me."

She scoffed, "How can that be? I'm the one who 'ruined' you."

"It's one of the perplexities of life."

She laughed at him. "You have an answer for everything."

"No. You do. The answer to all my needs." And he kissed her more seriously.

She was indulgent, wiggling and getting comfortable as his hands and body moved, and he became more intent. This time he had the opportunity to pay more attention, the time to enjoy, the leisure to explore. And he did. It was a while before he caught her attention, but he did. And then she helped. She teased and tempted, and he loved it. So did she. She was so new to such encounters that she thought she was very bold and inventive, and she was curious. He helped her to learn, and he learned with her. They spent that time in loving, and they slept together.

She awoke in the morning to find him watching her, and she smiled. He leaned to kiss her, and his hands were on her. She giggled. She'd never giggled, but she did then. And she allowed him to love her lavishly, however briefly. He'd coaxed, "Let me just go ahead. I need you desperately, and I've always dreamed of waking and taking a willing woman. Be willing with me."

She lay back and welcomed him. And he moved over her and pressed into her as he luxuriated in the act. He sighed and moved and stretched and swirled with great, satisfying pleasure.

Replete, he leaned up on his elbows and smiled down at her. He kissed her sweetly and said, "Thank you. Did I leave you hungry? I can fix any problem."

"No. I'm fine. I find you interesting."

"Any parts more interesting than others?"

"I'm from a family of girls. So men are strange to me. I find your mind fascinating."

He raised his eyebrows in great surprise. "Not my body?"

She ran her hand over his shoulder and along what she could reach between his hairy chest and her flattened breasts. "Your body is spectacular. I would like to stare at you."

"Any time."

"I've always been so *curious*. But it's not easy to go up to a man who is completely dressed and busy, to ask him if he'd mind taking off his clothes just so I can look at him. He could get the idea I was trying to come on to him."

"Quite possibly."

"Would you mind if I look at you?"

"Be my guest."

"I have to take the covers off."

"What men have to do for voracious women is just shocking."

"I just want to look."

"Yeah. Sure. Then you'll want to touch. Then you'll want to lick. And who knows what else?"

"I'll try to be gentle."

"Mother warned me about women like you. Saying they are curious and then taking advantage of my trying to be helpful and kind. Whoops! That tickles."

With exaggerated patience she asked, "Do you mind? You're supposed to be lying still. I have hardly begun. Just be calm."

After a silent minute he exclaimed, "You *are* curious!" He drew in a long, surprised breath. "Do that again."

"That."

"Where did you learn to do that?"

"You did it to me last night. And this."

His fingers dug into the sheet and mattress. "Do that again." And later he begged, "Again."

But she climbed up over him, slid down on him and leaned over to rub herself on his hairy chest. His arms came around her and his mouth hunted hers. After he'd kissed her silly, he sought another packet.

Then he turned her over on her back and made love to her. He made her squeal and struggle. He teased her and separated from her. Then she coaxed, and he tempted her. Finally she pushed him over and climbed back on top of him and rode him. He loved it. His hands helped her to move and gave her the pressure she wanted. And having reached the zenith, she collapsed on him and couldn't move.

He was very tender with her. He slid over and put her into his heated place in the bed, and released her from their coupling. Then he left the bed and covered her. And she slept.

He brought in an enormous breakfast. He'd cut a cardboard box out on the long sides to make a bed tray, and he'd fixed cereal, poached eggs and fried bacon with a stack of toast. He handed her a warm wash-cloth to rub over her face and hand, and he piled the pillows behind her back and gave her a sweater to put around her naked chest.

"How do you know how to do all this? I thought you didn't have much experience. I think you've fooled me. No man knows to do this."

"I've had to be cared for. Twice, I was almost killed—once by a fall and once by a bull on a farm. I am twice a walking miracle. I must have been allowed to live so that I could find you."

She frowned at him. "How did you fall?"

"My dad and I were on the barn roof, and I fell off. It's a miracle that I lived. The barn roof was about forty feet high. I fell flat. They thought I was dead then. They gave me mouth-to-mouth, and I breathed. And the emergency medics told me later that they thought taking me in was a waste of time. But I lived. No one could ever figure out how."

"And the bull?"

"He was a pet. But that day he ran amok, and he gored me. You had to've noticed the scar. They had some trouble stuffing me back inside. Sorry. It was another time they thought they were wasting their efforts. My dad was dead then. I was the youngest and the only one left at home. It was a miracle.''

"Your poor mother.''

"She's a good, strong woman. But she still misses my dad. They had a great love." He smiled at her, there in his bed, and he said softly, "This, too, is a miracle, and I know how nice it is to be cosseted when you're tired. You must be worn-out. I've been too greedy with you.''

She gave him a heavy-lidded look. "That last time was all my idea.''

"But you wanted a quick one, the way I had you, and I prolonged my own pleasure and made you wait.''

She smiled wickedly. "I wasn't complaining at any time.''

"I can't believe these last fourteen hours. I think I could die happy. I feel as if you are a man's last wish.''

"What a gloomy thought. Don't be silly. Help me eat all this.''

He sat down on the side of the bed which tilted the tray and they both had to grab glasses and plates. He sat more carefully, and although he said he'd already eaten, he did help her.

He felt he was in heaven. He stood around that day and the next, smiling at her. On Sunday he watched her as he leaned against walls, or sat, or stood.

"Quit that." She laughed. "You make me self-conscious.''

"You're beautiful. I like to watch you move. You jiggle. I like it that you don't wear a bra around—''

She snapped her head down. "I jiggle?''

"Didn't you realize that? I thought you went bra-less to entice me.''

"I went braless because it's so hellish to hook the blamed things with this stupid cast. Don't be distracted by an innocent, unaware jiggle," she declared virtuously. "I meant nothing by it."

"You don't want to entice me?" He looked genuinely hurt.

"Not right now." But she went to him and stretched up his body and kissed him, leaning into him, and she smiled at him.

"Don't wear a bra. Promise me that after they take off the cast, you won't put on a bra."

"I'll take your request under advisement."

"A man can't ask for much more." He hugged her tightly and closed his eyes under the wave of amazement that he was there, on earth, and that she was in his arms willingly.

As she was throwing together a meat loaf in the kitchen and he was standing around admiring her, he asked her, "Do you believe that you've had other lives?"

"I've never had the time to worry about it."

"Do you believe in reincarnation?"

She shrugged. "People seem to."

"Do you think we could have known each other in another time?"

"I have enough to think about in this one. I really don't care whether or not I lived in another time. That was then. This is now."

"How do you like 'now'?"

"Busy. Sometimes I do wonder what will happen to our planet. This land is such a marvel that it would be a shame to ruin it. It could take eons for the land to recover from our carelessness, and maybe never again could it support life as we know it. That would be a terrible thing." She threw an empty ketchup bottle into the trash and opened cupboards, looking for another.

"Yeah. But what about us? What do you think about . . . us?"

"This is amazing for a first affair. I never thought I would do anything so rash as to have one, but for a first one, this is just marvelous."

He was stunned. A *first* affair? What did she mean, a *first one*? That implied there would be others. "You plan on having a series? Like a serial killer?"

"How would I know? I never dreamed of getting involved this time. You've taken me by surprise." She found a bottle of ketchup in the bottom of the broom closet.

"And then some other guy will come along and 'take you by surprise,' and you'll jump into bed with him?"

She *considered* that. She didn't immediately scoff, or come to him and put her arms around him to comfort him. No—she considered it.

She said, "I'm really terribly involved with my work. I think most people decide how they want to spend their lives, and they set goals. My work has no real foreseeable results. What we're working on is a hundred years away, a thousand years, ten thousand years. If we don't work on it now, there will be no future for this land. So my petty desires, stacked up against that, are really inconsequential."

"We aren't going to get married?" he asked in real shock.

"Good gravy, Graham, we hardly know each other. You're jumping whole gobs of time down the line. I never intended to begin an affair, much less consider marriage." She turned to look at him very seriously. "Perhaps it would be better if we set this attraction and its ramifications aside and see what happens." She struggled with the cap of the ketchup bottle.

"You call me a ramification?" He was offended.

She studied him. "You're a very attractive, very sweet man. I wish that I could be a different woman for you."

"I don't want a 'different' woman. I want you."

She became restless. "You're a complication in my life. I never dreamed I could give up difficult women apartment-sharers to have even more trouble with a man sharing this place. You're a complication I don't need." She was pleading, not nasty.

He was a "difficult ramification" that was a "complication." He looked at his shoes and frowned.

She went on with something like irritation. "I thought I was safe with you because I've never cared for blonds."

He raised his brown gaze and just looked at her. She gave no thought to him as a man. He was a safe blond ramification who was simply a complication in her life. She offended him.

He took the bottle from her, opened it and handed it back. She splatted some into the meat-loaf mixture and set the bottle aside, then began to squash the mess together with her good hand.

He watched her earnestly mixing the meat loaf, jiggling, concentrated, dedicated. She was a precious woman. She just needed to realize that as little as past lives mattered, the present was paramount. They needed to concentrate on now and not on what might happen in the future—the let's-live-for-today attitude. He shifted to begin speaking, and the doorbell rang.

Seven

It was almost six weeks that Graham had shared her apartment, but it was the first time the doorbell had rung. Graham knew that she had friends, but they were the ones she saw at work. Because her life was different, she was rarely at the complex, where she had lived for almost two years.

He saw that Roberta was equally surprised by the doorbell. She said, "It isn't Maintenance. It must be for you."

Graham was annoyed by the interruption and went to the door to dispatch whoever it was, so that he could reconcile Roberta to their commitment. He had to make her see that they belonged together, and that he was no "first" affair.

So he opened the door in a dismissive way. And there stood Jim McFarland.

Graham stared.

Jim smiled a little and stood waiting to be invited inside. He was shaved and combed and neat-looking. Graham had never seen Jim so tidy. Graham frowned at his mentor and asked, "Why are you here?"

"No Hello or How are you? Just Why?"

"We understand each other."

"I brought you a file. It's the Mullins case."

"I could get it tomorrow."

"I have to go to Utah. There's been an air crash with civilian damage. I need to brief you on a couple of things. May I come in, or do you want to stand here and discuss this?"

"Let's go out to your car."

Jim smiled in such a way that Graham knew the interloper did understand that Graham didn't want him around Roberta.

Graham turned to call to Roberta that he'd be back in a minute, and there she was, right beside him. Small, lovely, smiling. No bra.

She said, "Come in."

Jim smiled a little and gave Graham a quick glance. Then he said to Roberta, "I'm not interrupting?"

"Of course not. I'm Roberta Lambert."

"We've met a couple of times. I'm Jim McFarland."

Then Roberta won Graham's heart. She said, "Graham's friend. He speaks so nicely of you."

That surprised both men. Jim gave a glinting smile at Graham. If Graham hadn't been so furiously possessive, he would have seen the humor, too, but he did not.

Like a strange dog in another dog's territory, Jim came slowly inside, and Roberta closed the door. It was

she who invited Jim to sit down, and he did. Graham
stood, unwelcoming.

Curious, Roberta looked from one to the other before she suggested, "You must have business? If you're
here to arrest Graham, I'm an attorney and an environmentalist, and he must be preserved, so you'll have
to deal with me."

While she spoke, Graham watched Jim like a hawk.
He saw the way Jim's focus was on Roberta and Graham saw the fleetingly revealed depths of Jim's need as
she said that he would have to deal with her.

Graham wasn't flattered by her defense of him. It
was charming, but she'd be equally concerned for that
damned condor. He couldn't believe her protective instincts for him were emotionally personal; he was just
included under her umbrella. And, being male, he was
a little ticked off that she didn't think he was capable
of handling his own protection—and hers. That was
what he was doing—standing there, guarding the en-
virons from this interloper.

He already knew how Jim felt about Roberta, but
Jim had given her to him. Graham had told Jim right
away that he had one last and final chance, which Jim
had declined. What was he doing there? "What are you
doing here?"

Roberta gave a little gasp of surprise, but Jim
understood the question exactly. He looked at Graham kindly and replied gently, "I just wondered
how...you were doing."

"Fine."

Roberta frowned at Graham and cocked her head as
she tried to figure him out. She felt the undercurrents
but didn't understand them. She said, "Well, I'll go
finish the meat loaf." She turned back at the end of the

wall that separated the living room from the kitchen area and asked, "Can you stay?"

His stare on Jim, Graham answered, "Not this time."

Roberta's glance rested on Graham for a long second, then she smiled at Jim and said, "Perhaps another time."

He'd half risen when she had moved to leave the room and now he settled back. "Thank you. Perhaps."

Both men were silent as Roberta went back into the kitchen and turned on the radio to a music station. Jim looked at Graham, who remained standing. Silent, Jim rubbed his face with both hands, and the weariness of the movement got to Graham. He went over to sit on a chair next to the sofa and wait.

With a sigh, Jim said, "On the Mullins case. In *Shepherd's Citations*, I found a group of cases that may have some bearing on the issue. None has been overturned. I photocopied them." He took the papers from his briefcase. "I think you'll find this interesting. The guy's a cheat. With this angle, you may chip away at him."

They were speaking quietly so that their voices wouldn't carry. Graham asked, "Why did you take this time on a weekend?"

Jim replied slowly, "I needed the distraction."

He stood up, handing the papers to Graham. "I've arranged to travel for a week or so. Take care. Tell Roberta...tell her...thank her for the invitation to supper."

Graham nodded once and stood. Jim offered his hand. Almost reluctantly, Graham took it. Then he looked into Jim's troubled gray eyes, put an arm

around him and hugged him. They parted awkwardly
and went to the door silently. Graham opened it, and
Jim nodded once before he left.

Graham was closing the door firmly, thoughtfully,
when Roberta came around the end of the wall. "He's
gone already?"

"He just dropped off some papers."

"He seems to be a nice man."

"He is."

Roberta watched Graham for a minute, then she
asked, "Want a salad with the meat loaf?"

"I'll fix it."

"Are you okay?"

"Yeah." He went to the door of his room and
opened it. "Anything needs doing, come get me, I'm
going to play the keyboard."

"Can't I hear?"

"I'll put it on audio."

The pieces he chose to play were emotional and tumultuous. His music expressed his disappointment in
Roberta's casual treatment of their magic. He loved
Roberta. And Jim was his friend. Graham understood
Jim's belated regret, but Graham couldn't give up his
try for Roberta. Life was tough. He played well, and he
felt the music through his body.

In the kitchen Roberta felt not only the music, but
Graham's torment. What was between Jim and Graham? Some problem. She went to him.

Graham had an adjustable stool that he sat on, and
the keyboard was on folding legs. He was concentrated on the music. His body moved with it. He was
really magnificent.

She crawled into his bed and pulled the spread over
her, lying there, listening, as absorbed as he.

He came to the end of the piece and touched the last lingering note. One hand dropped to his lap, and he turned to see her there.

He stared at her, realizing she was on his bed. It was an emotional encounter of just their shared awareness. Then he stood up, still watching her, and he took off his clothes. He came to her and lifted back the cover, and she turned so that her shoulders were flat while she lay on one hip. Her body was very femininely curved.

He took off the fuzzy slippers and pulled off the yellow lounge pants. Then he separated her knees, pulled her astraddle him and took off her top. He crushed her bare body to his and he kissed her. His kiss was as emotional and tumultuous as his playing had been, and they made silent love.

He consumed her. His movements were as deliberate as his playing of the music, and he drew responses from her depths that stunned her. His blond hair was tousled, and yellow flames leaped in his brown eyes. His face was gaunt and serious, his eyes burned into her, and he was scorchingly hot. His muscles were hard as iron, and his hands were demanding—as demanding of her as they'd been of the keyboard. And she gave him what he wanted, what he needed. She gave him comfort, the feeling of living, the feeling of possession.

He went to sleep, but Roberta lay awake, troubled, watching this marvelous, complicated man by her side, his hands still holding her. And she felt her heart touched by him. She had never experienced anything to compare to listening to that magnificent music, played by him, and then being the recipient of such re-

markable love, shared with him. She was overwhelmed.

For a long time she lay there, watching him, learning him. And then she, too, fell asleep.

They smelled the meat loaf when they wakened. It
was in the conventional oven, which had no timer. The
loaf was a hard, unrecognizable lump. The baked po-
tatoes looked as if they'd come from an ancient dig.

They had a boxed Italian spaghetti, with sliced
olives, parsley and mushrooms added, and they made
garlic bread. They opened wine and savored the meal.
He told her about the Mullins case, and they read the
photocopies Jim had brought to Graham. She said,
"Mullins is a crook."

"Yes."

"I hope you win. I'm a taxpayer and I hate cheats."

"Jim did a brilliant job of finding this particular
slant. It'll help. It makes the case more thorough. He's
a formidable opponent."

" 'Opponent'? You make Jim seem like he's on the
other side."

Of course, Jim was. He'd wanted Roberta. And he
couldn't quite stay away from her. Graham was troubled by Jim's attraction to Roberta, even as he rejected his competition. And with it all, Roberta
thought of Graham as a "first" affair.

Would Jim be her second?

Graham was jealous. God, but he was jealous! Such
a petty emotion. No civilized man should feel such a
primitive reaction to another man. Jim would keep his
distance. He'd deliberately chosen not to pursue Roberta. But Jim had found this excuse to come over and
glimpse her. And look at the excuse Jim had dug out.

Graham would probably win the case, just because Jim was so lured by Roberta that he'd needed an excuse to see her, just to look at her. Graham could understand it.

He looked at Roberta sitting next to him in her dining room, and he leaned and kissed the spaghetti sauce off her mouth. It was excessively sensual, for he did it slowly, meticulously and erotically. It was the beginning of a long session of making love to her. And his manner was different, yet again.

He was tender, considerate. And he saw to it that she was sensuously pleasured. He was so concerned with her that he was more deliciously erotic than he'd ever been. He wasn't loving her for effect, but to affect. His passionate concern wasn't contrived.

They slept together that night, in his bed. In the morning she was wakened by his alarm and lay there, watching him get ready to go to work. He made the coffee and brought her a cup, then undressed and got back into bed with her, so that they both had to scramble to make work on time. He laughed then, for the first time in almost twenty-four hours.

When Roberta finally got to shed her cast, Graham had to hold her hand and kiss it, because he wasn't familiar with it, and since it had been protected from him, it had never received its share of his attention. She laughed at him. He held her hand.

In those last weeks of February, it seemed one or the other of them was out of town. Their reunions were hungry, and they made love so ravenously that they barely spoke. She arranged for them to go one weekend to Florida, to an aunt's condo overlooking the Atlantic. No one had rented it for that weekend, and the aunt allowed Roberta to have it to herself—her and Graham.

Their plane was met by Jeffrey, the houseman, and Graham found the apartment was enormous. A housekeeping couple also came with the place. Meals simply appeared, and the weather was gloriously different from D.C. They saw some whales spouting, out in the water, and Roberta became quite strung out over them. She wanted to go out in a boat to see them and to touch them, but Graham said they were too big, and she shouldn't bother them. They ought to be left in peace. She could understand that. They gathered shells, they saw porpoises, and they fed the gulls.

They drove her aunt's car down the coast to see the lookout hills made solely of clam shells long, long ago by ancient people who'd lived in that land. And having just gathered a modest pile of seashells, Graham and Roberta agreed that any mound of clamshells over a hundred feet high took one hell of a lot of clams.

But they stood on top of one, on a platform the park system had provided, and they looked out over the beautiful coastal lands with the ocean beyond and the inland waters just below them. The sun was out, and the ocean breeze was mild and refreshing. It was a beautiful place to live.

Roberta said, "Think of a warning system that is limited to only how far your eyes can see."

"There had to be warning systems, even then," Graham pointed out. He wanted to remind her how long people had survived.

"But their wars didn't ruin the land for all time."

There was no answer to that.

They swam in one of the complex's outdoor, heated pools, and smiled over the insane luxury of it. They explored places to eat and climbed one of the last of the lighthouses. They played hide-and-seek in that enormous apartment, and she was surprised to find he wouldn't accept crossed fingers as a King's X, a time out, in this democracy.

She laughed when he told her what the forfeit was, and expressed great amazement. But he collected—on the carpet, before the opened sliding doors and the balcony that overlooked the ocean. With the curtains billowing gently, and the winds benign, they made lovely, passionate love.

They left regretfully. It had been an idyll, a time out of time. A memory. She spoke of it that way, with sweet regret. And she froze his heart.

It was on the first of March that she gave the first party since he'd been there. She asked him to include some of his friends, and he did select several men he knew, because she had an excess of women friends, naturally. But it also seemed like a good time to include the woman vet who'd taken care of Gus.

He dropped by the vet's office to see Gus. He found the mouse was ensconced as sort of a welcoming mayor in the reception room. Gus had a magnificent new cage, with varying levels. He greeted Graham with a trilling of enthusiasm and came to the wires to tell his old friend all that was going on. The people waiting were entranced, and Graham laughed.

It wasn't long before the vet was there beside him. Mildred Phillips smiled up at Graham and waited. He realized she was expecting to be asked out, and that made him feel bad. He shook his head a little and said, "We're giving a party. There'll be some interesting people there, and I just wondered if you'd like to join us."

She looked down at her hands, then looked up and smiled as she said, "I'd be delighted."

He gave her his card. She held it in both her hands. And he wondered if he'd been kind. "I see you haven't been able to foist Gus off onto anybody."

"Everyone loves him. I couldn't give him to someone else."

"For a street mouse, he's really come up in the world."

"Not many sing, and when he does, as he's doing now, no one believes it. It's really very nice. It cheers the dog and cat patients no end."

He grinned down at her. "Want me to go out and thrash the streets for more singing mice?"

"No."

"Come to our party. A couple of my friends will be there, and you can look them over. Don't say anything about Gus."

She shook her head chidingly.

He coaxed. "We'll see you Saturday about six. It's a snacking supper party. A little booze or whatever. Come prepared to eat. I assume you're called Milly?"

She nodded.

"See you then. So long, Gus."

Gus trilled after him, all the way out the door.

The lovers had a quick, hard day preparing for their gathering. Some of the nibbles were prepared by a caterer. Graham wanted to pay for it all, but they split the cost as Roberta insisted. Graham relished the sharing of the work. He saw to it that he did most of it, but it was doing it with Roberta that he treasured.

She accepted the day as no big deal. That sobered him. He wondered if she thought of him that way.

Something like a party: a lot of work and some pleasure.

He was troubled by her response to him. She could
be so loving, but the closeness didn't carry over into
their lives. He didn't want a woman who clung to his
arm twenty-four hours a day, but he did want one who
enjoyed being around him. One who preferred his
company to anyone else's, one who loved him, a
woman with whom he came first.

As their friends arrived, Graham was especially sensitive to relationships. He watched and listened. There
weren't very many couples who had what he wanted.
Were his expectations unreasonable?

Had his parents' marriage and love been too ideal?
Had they had something together that was not realis-
tic in this time? *Commitment*—that was probably the
key word.

He could remember his father blazing mad at his
mother, but there had never been the fear that they'd
tear up the family. It was just...anger. They hadn't
verbally abused each other. Their quarrels had stayed
on whatever had made them mad.

Graham never remembered either of them threaten-
ing the other, or saying anything nasty about the other,
nothing belittling or derogatory. They had been a team,
even when they were mad as hell.

They had always made up in a day or two; sometimes it had taken a little longer. They'd be careful for
a while, then they'd laugh and tease, mending the rip
in their relationship. His mother would sass and his dad
would laugh, and they'd flirt. The kids would all laugh,
too, and the house would be back to normal.

They had all helped their mother as she'd grieved for
their dad. It had been a terrible thing. But his mother

hadn't railed at God or blamed Him. There was a waiting in her, as it used to be when his dad was late getting home. That was the kind of love Graham wanted. He had it for Roberta.

But what about her? Maybe he wasn't the other half of a whole to her.

Was . . . was Jim her other half? What if Jim didn't realize that Graham and Roberta were the only two people who could complete each other? What if Roberta needed Jim to complete her life? Could Graham give her up to Jim now, after he'd known her?

His turmoil over rejecting such a thought boiled over then, and he couldn't think straight, because his love for Roberta got in the way. He knew only that he loved her; that he wanted her as his other half. And he suffered.

Graham saw that Milly came a little late, as most strangers did when they went to a party where they didn't know anyone. Graham introduced her to Roberta, who said, "Now how in the world did Graham ever meet a veterinarian?" She laughed. "Trust him to find a beautiful woman."

And Graham's gaze loved Roberta for so easily giving that compliment to Milly.

Graham's friends arrived, and they added to the pleasant tone of the party. They brought out Graham's keyboard and two of them played exuberantly. Not as skilled as Graham, but they enjoyed it and were noisy, and they could play the party tunes that everyone knew how to sing.

In passing, Roberta said to Graham, "I'm glad I didn't hire anyone. Who could beat them? You're brilliant."

The glow of that lasted until he realized he wasn't really the receiver of her compliment.

When did Jim arrive? Later Graham tried to remember. Everything was rather nicely hazy, and with an electric shock, Graham realized that Jim McFarland was at their party. How?

Graham was so stricken that he couldn't bring himself to confront Jim. He didn't even want to face Roberta, because he knew that somehow fate had double-crossed him, and Jim was there for Roberta. Graham considered just leaving. He could go to a motel, and then sometime during the late afternoon on Monday, he could come back to pack up and leave. There were just things that no man fought.

He saw that Jim never turned away from Roberta. No matter where she was, his body faced toward her. He appeared to talk to people, and he appeared not to be watching her, but if that was so, why did his body face her way? Did they feel something so powerful that they couldn't resist? It pulled them together, and they were helpless? How had he gotten between such people? What had he ever done to deserve this?

He was suffering so that the sounds around him didn't quite register in his mind. Milly asked him if anything was wrong, if he felt all right. He said he was fine. Why couldn't he have loved her? She noticed he was under stress.

Then Roberta came to him. She smiled at him as if nothing at all was the matter and said, "Have you talked to Jim?"

Miserably he looked at his love. What did Jim have to say? That Graham was to move out so that Jim could move in? Graham couldn't draw his stare from his love, and she said, "Graham? Are you okay? You aren't angry that he's here, are you?"

Angry? No. Killed by it? Probably. Now he began to understand his mother's waiting. She was just putting in time on this earth. But she functioned, she contributed. He could do that. He said, "No. I believe I understand."

"See if you can't make up your quarrel. I don't know what's wrong between you two, but when I ran into Jim at a senator's fund-raising yesterday, I thought maybe if you two just saw each other here, you could smooth things out. He's leaving, you know. He's going to England."

"And you? Where will you be?" His soul was naked in his dead eyes.

"Where will *I* be? Where do you think? I'll be here." She frowned at him as if he might have had too much to drink, then she went on through their crush of guests.

England? Jim was to go to England. Graham worked his way over to where Jim stood, and Jim turned to him. If Jim had won, his gray eyes showed no triumph. Graham asked, "England?"

Jim nodded. "It was as far away as I could manage without going to Lebanon."

"Will she be joining you?"

"Who?"

Graham's glance instantly found Roberta. "She."

"God, man, what has your imagination done to you? She doesn't realize I have this thing about her. She thinks you and I've had a misunderstanding. She asked me to come here tonight so that we can straighten it out before I leave. She cares about you. She knows we're friends. She wants us to stay friends. She has no idea she's the cause of this thing between us, this jealousy. If . . ."

"Then . . ." Graham couldn't breathe.

"I'm leaving in the morning. I've managed a staff appointment. It's a beginning. It's what I thought I wanted. Look, Graham, I'll have what I want. You're with her. I'm not sure you have her full attention yet, but she does care about you. All you have to do is appear more important than the impact of waste that's poisonous for ten thousand years. That may take a little doing."

And Graham's voice cracked. "What about you?"

"Maybe I'll catch up with her in another lifetime. I never caught her eye the way you did. She turned me down and didn't remember meeting me. Remember that."

Much, much later, when word got out that Jim McFarland was leaving for England in the morning, those at the keyboard played "Auld Lang Syne," and everyone sang the words. They were all a little mellow by then, and the women lined up to kiss Jim goodbye. Roberta was one, and every nerve in Graham's body watched.

When their lips met, would lightning flash? Would thunder roar and the heavens split? Would she *know*? Jim had seen she was in line. He lingered, then, with each woman, teasing and hugging her closely, so when Roberta's turn came he could take her into his arms, to kiss her and hold her.

Nothing happened. Roberta laughed and wiggled free and mussed his hair. She stood with the others and watched, then looked around for Graham. When she saw his face, hers stilled, and she came immediately to him. "Didn't you make up your quarrel? You still look angry."

"I love you, Roberta."

She laughed. "You silly." And she leaned against him sweetly, willingly. And she kissed him lingeringly.

It was Graham who broke from her. He finally lifted his mouth from her soft kiss, raised his head a little and saw that Jim watched. Jim smiled just a little and winked as he nodded a couple of small times as if he was saying, See? What did I tell you?

Roberta said, "Go out and walk to his car with him. If he has caught a woman's attention, she'll be going along. But Jim won't mind you going that far. Tell him goodbye."

But Jim left alone. He was out of the room before Graham caught up with him, and was already turning the corner of the building when Graham whistled. Jim stopped and waited.

They didn't say anything. But they shook hands and then put their arms around each other and stood grieving for their lost companionship. Their lives had been changed by a woman who didn't even realize it.

Graham stood by the parking area and watched Jim drive away, and then he was alone. He took a deep breath and wondered at all the tangled emotions that people must endure. He put his hands into his trouser pockets and turned—to brush against Roberta, who stood waiting for him.

"How long have you been here?"

She looked past him at the parking lot. "Is he gone?"

"Yes."

"Did you two make up?"

"We hugged each other."

"Why were you estranged?"

He noted the word. She realized the nuance. "Some day I shall tell you."

"I'm glad you parted friends."

"Me, too."

"Here's your jacket. Let's walk around the track once. Our guests won't miss us at all."

Graham smiled in the night.

Eight

It was as they walked around the track that night, that Graham began to get a glimmer into the whys and wherefores of Roberta Lambert.

She held his hand, and she talked to him. Gradually Graham realized she meant to ease his sadness about his friend's leaving. She thought his distress was from his association with Jim.

But how could he explain to her, without confessing that Jim loved her? That Jim was a competitor for her against his own will, and that he had left the country in order to free himself of her? How would she take that?

For a woman to know a man cared for her, to such lengths, would act as an aphrodisiac. At the very least, it would capture her compassion. Every woman knew she was worth that kind of love.

But, Graham fretted, should the fact that Roberta was more important to him than his own career make his love fade in comparison to Jim's rather selfish and dramatic rejection of love? No. Nothing could be gained by telling Roberta why Jim had left the country, or that Graham figured in the whole scene in a very minor and inadvertent part.

However, all egos can use stroking. And for a woman to know she had tempted a dedicated man from his chosen path, would be a heady thing for her. Graham should tell her. But when? Surely not now, when she was calling Graham her "first" affair.

So, as he and Roberta walked the jogging path's circuit, her small hand nestled in his large warm one, Graham decided he would tell her on their fiftieth wedding anniversary.

What if he didn't survive that long? His father hadn't. It would be a shame for a woman never to know about the devotion of a might-have-been. He'd write it all down and include it with his will. Not many women can command that kind of love and not even know about it. She ought to know...but not for a long, long time.

He tuned in to hear Roberta saying, "So my sister, George, has become involved with him. The whole family is on their ear. He isn't at all suitable. When Tate—she's the eldest—called me to tell me about it, she said, 'Guess what. Do you know what Quintus Finnig has done?' Well, he's such a smoky character that I said, 'The Feds have him, and Graham will have to defend the government against him.' She said, 'Who is Graham?' That Tate never lets anything go by her. By now, all the Lamberts know I know a man named Graham Rawlins.''

"Who is Quintus Finnig, and why will I be opposing him?"

"Heaven only knows. He's a shadowy character in Chicago who has too wide an acquaintance to be pure, and he's been involved with three of my sisters—no, not that way—but somehow he's tangled up in just about everything. Now George is in love with him. That's Georgina, she's the next older to me, and they are *probably* going to get married, if Daddy holds still for it. I'm running out of single sisters. This will leave just Fred and me unmarried. In one year three Lambert sisters have taken the leap. Can you believe that?"

Roberta would be four, if Graham had anything to do with it. All he needed was a little cooperation.

Then Roberta slid in, "Tell me about Milly. She's a veterinarian. How long have you known her?"

"I met her just after I met you."

"Oh?"

"Does your dad think Finnig is a crook?"

"I have no idea. Both my brothers-in-law vouch for him in a sort of hands-off way. I know that's a dubious clearance, but they can't seem to find anything really *wrong* about him. And George loves him. That alone recommends him. George is a darling. But then—" she gave him a flirting look "—all the Lambert sisters are darling."

"One of them is a witch."

"Which one? Not Tate. She was something of a tomboy as a child. I think the only one who would qualify as a witch would be Fred, and she's so namby-pamby that she wouldn't have the intestinal fortitude to do anything wicked."

"You have a sister who is namby-pamby?"

"We don't understand it, either. George thinks it's because Tate bullied Fred so much as an impressionable child. Fred's two years younger than Tate. During Tate's Tarzan period, Fred was Jane. George was Cheetah, and I was a native. Hillary was Boy, Tarzan's found son. Tate made Fred stand around screaming for help for two years—so Tarzan could rescue her—and we think it marked Fred. It made her believe she should be helpless, while she stood around waiting for someone to show up and save her. Did you ever play that way?"

"I farmed from the time I could crawl. Then I worked out, played football and studied, when Mother didn't have me chained to the piano. I never had time for anything else."

"You must have fooled around a little, you take to it so well."

"A green farm boy, in the big city, with a woman who took advantage of his innocence."

"I assume you are speaking of me? How can you possibly figure *I* had any experience?"

"Well, somebody sure gave me an in-depth experience." He put his hand on the back of her nape and shook her a little. Then he kissed her, in depth.

When he lifted his mouth she asked, "How did you meet Milly?"

He blinked and replied glibly, "Through a friend. We need to go back in and see to it no one's doing anything they oughtn't. We haven't been the best of chaperons."

So they went inside to a pleasant party that was still crowded and a little noisy and very casual. People had opened Graham's doors, made use of his bathroom, and there was an overflow of people sitting on his bed, desk and chair and leaning against his walls. The party really needed more space. But no one had opened Roberta's door. It was still sealed from any stranger. Graham thought that was as it should be. When the bastion was breached, he would do it.

Milly was laughing with some of Graham's friends, and since she was still there, it was apparent she was enjoying the party. He looked at Milly rather nostalgically. She was a nice, uncomplicated woman who had invited his regard. Why couldn't he have settled for an uncomplicated woman? Why set himself to the chore it would take to make Roberta realize she belonged to him and have her accept it gladly? He sighed and looked away—into Roberta's measuring eyes.

After that, he found her looking at him or standing near to him quite often. He smiled and winked at her across other people, or he leaned and kissed her cheek when she was close by. But she studied him.

It just so happened that he was around the living-room wall, in the kitchen-dining area, when he heard Roberta talking to Milly. Graham moved a little so that he could see them, but Roberta's back was to Graham. Their talk was the usual "Where's your home, where did you get your training, how did you end up in D.C.?" But his ears perked up when Roberta asked, "Graham tells me you met through a friend. Who was that?"

With no hesitation at all, Milly said, "Gus. He has an unusual voice."

That was bad enough, but when Roberta said, "I don't believe I know him."

With a brief flick of a droll glance at Graham, and as smooth as silk, Milly replied, "I'm sure you've met him at least once."

Graham had lifted his glass to take a sip. Milly's words took him by surprise and he choked. Milly came around the corner to solicitously pound on his back, while Roberta looked concerned and got him a tissue and held his arm up.

He managed a glinting look at Milly, chiding her wickedness, but she showed no remorse at all. She even had the audacity to smile rather smugly. That almost set him off again.

Some of their guests didn't leave until after two in the morning. They had helped to clean up, and they went on talking. It was a good party. Graham's friends had added a nice seasoning. They'd coaxed some of the women into staying, and Milly was one. Martin seemed to favor Milly, and she allowed that.

So it was almost three when the last of them left the place, in rather tidy condition. The two hosts stood in the doorway with a hushing of the goodbyes, and then they were alone.

"You give good parties, Miss Lambert."

"So do you, Mr. Rawlins. Why didn't you invite Gus?"

"He-e-e...couldn't get away." But he wasn't as smooth as Milly, and he had to bite his lip.

They turned out the lights, and he took her into his room to make sweet and tender love to her. Standing next to the bed, he took off his clothes as she watched. Naked, he reached to enclose her against him to feel the silk of her dress against his susceptible skin. He bent his head down to seek her mouth and kiss her exquisitely. He put his roughened, callused hands on her head and gently pushed his long fingers into the tumbled mass of silken threads as he slowly mussed the marvel of her hair around her shoulders. He took off her clothes little by little, teasing her and himself as he discovered new and amazing delights that had to be admired and examined and cherished.

He loved her. His eyes, his hands, his mouth, his body loved her. He held her to his heat and groaned with his love. His big hands smoothed her hair from her face and his hot eyes looked down at her with the flames burning there. His mouth scorched hers, and he breathed a furnace breath against her throat.

He made her wait. Her little hands and the strength of her arms only charmed him and curled his passion tighter. She deliberately rubbed against his differently textured body with its hard planes and dark, wiry hair. She pushed her fingers into his thick blond hair and held his head to her as she squirmed and gasped. But still he made her wait.

He lifted her and carried her around the room, and then into the living room, where he put her on the sofa and sat beside her to touch and feel and knead and kiss her. She became lax and malleable as she sighed and gasped, and languorously moved, and allowed him his way.

He ran his fingers along her smooth and silken surface, and then used his palm as he listened to the faint sound of it on her, watching as he did that. He cupped and lifted her breast, moving his hand as he curled his fingers to capture the weight and squeeze it lightly. Then he bent his head to kiss the roundness, before he touched his tongue to the tip. His mouth engulfed the nub and pulled it longer, deeper into his mouth, caressing with his tongue, stroking on the underside, driving her wild.

She began to make small sounds and her body writhed coaxingly. Her knee bent up over his hip and the inside of her thigh and calf rubbed along his hip and down the different feel of his hairy thigh.

He pulled her across his chest as he sat sprawled and wide-kneed, fastening his greedy mouth on hers in deep kisses. With his big hands under her armpits, his thumbs at the front of her shoulders, his wrists pressed into the softness, pushing her breasts together, he slowly rubbed her chest against his, maneuvering her body to pressure his and thrill him down his length.

She breathed deeply of him—his heat, his man smell, his particular fragrance. She wiggled to get closer, and her body was warmed by his fevered one. Their breaths were audible, and they were aware of the broken rhythms, of the sounds of their hands and the crinkling of the hairs that were rubbed together. The sounds of their mouths mating, sipping, sucking, his groans and pleasure rumbles, her squeaks and throat sounds. Their gazes met hotly—holding, serious, communicating. His kiss then was different. Gentle.

He lifted her aside to rise from the sofa, and she slid down supine, helpless, boneless, without his support. He stood above her, and as she looked up at him, his gaze went over her possessively. She was his. She didn't know it yet, but she was.

With superb muscle control, he leaned over, grasped her under her arms and lifted her slowly until he'd raised his arms up fully, holding her there above him. Then he slid her down him until their mouths met. And he held her there while he leisurely kissed her. Then he lifted her over his shoulder, and with one hand on her bare bottom, he carried his captive to his lair. She was his.

He laid her on his bed and watched her avidly as he rolled on the protection. Then he knelt over her in anticipation before he eased down into the nest of her ready, reaching arms and hands, her opened knees and her soft, eager body. He rubbed into her and took her slowly in one deep thrust. Deliciously he stroked her, loving her, holding her, murmuring to her, taking her up that narrowing spiral until she writhed with her need. And sweating, trembling, intensely concentrated, he laughed in his throat in his pleasure over her hungry desire as he took her out of the vortex, to the top of delight, and flew off with her into the convulsing starburst of passion, and they floated in the scattering rain of stars that were the throbbing aftershocks of thrills. She was his.

He pulled the covers up and they slept, locked together, pleasured, contented, sated. Until morning.

He wakened her with a caressing hand on her warm, lazy, stretching body. He smiled and said, "Good morning, my love."

"What a sneaky smile you wear, sir. I can only think you must want something of me, wearing a smile like that. Breakfast in bed?"

"Part of that's right."

"Uh." She made an elaborate show of thought. "Breakfast?"

"Not yet. But...something...in bed."

She lifted the covers and peeked down his body. "You're stark, staring naked! You need...clothing!"

"No, not exactly, but a form of that. I need a sheath. You."

She lay back dramatically. "Not that, again!"

"What do you mean, 'Again?' Like you just put up with me, you wicked woman. Look at my back, raked and furrowed by your clawing fingern—"

She snapped her head around. "I *hurt* you? Let me see. Surely, I couldn't have *hurt* you."

His eyes took on different lights because she was concerned for his welfare, his flesh. He laughed, very pleased, "I really don't mind. In fact, it rather pleases me that I could drive you that wild."

"But I didn't mean to hurt you. Let me see." She pulled at his shoulders, leaning across him, frowning.

In that position, of course he just wrapped his arms around her, pressed her down on him and began to nuzzle her throat, his hands moving coaxingly.

"Let me see your back."

"You have a back fetish? It's my front that's needy."

"How could you possibly want to make love again. Look at all I did just to get you to leave me alone last night so that I could go to sleep."

Remembering her passion, he laughed and scoffed, "You endured."

"Good heavens, yes. You don't think I'd want to do something that energetic and messy for fun, do you?"

"I did all the work."

"Baloney. You lay on top of me and let me do it all."

He laughed, remembering her writhing and squirming all curled around and urging him. He said falsely, "Poor girl."

"Woman."

"Female."

"Woman."

"All woman. And it so happens I'm a man. Give me your hand."

"I'll be darned. When did that happen?"

"I've been one all along."

"Phooey. I'd have noticed. You're really very stra— Wow, you still have some of that kind of kisses left after last night? That's incre—"

And with some wiggling and tickling and giggling, and some scuffling and wrestling, they romped around until the inevitable happened, and she was thoroughly pinned.

They lay at last, lax and contented, and they looked at each other and laughed. "Let me see your back."

"That's how all this started, woman." He slid from her gingerly, to lie beside her. "I can't go through that again today."

She laughed such a low and wicked sound that he had to laugh, too. But he wouldn't lift up and show her his back. And there was no way she could move him. He simply lay there and watched her, charmed and amused.

So she brought the exhausted victim breakfast in bed. Then she started to clean the apartment, and he showered, dressed and went to help. They worked well together. There was some small difference in the place after all their work; it was a little more straightened. But there wasn't even much in the vacuum bag.

"I've never yet had an apartmentmate who did a full share of the chores. You're terrific."

"You keep me around to *clean*?" He was indignant.

"What other possible reason could there be?" She was astonished.

He lunged, but she flipped aside and climbed onto the small of his back, astraddle him, so she could pull up his shirt and look for fingernail scratches. There were none. "You said—"

"Well, I *thought* that as wild as you were last night, I had to be in *shreds*." He turned over on the floor and lay with his arms behind his head, looking at her sitting on her heels.

She gestured to indicate the simple truth. "I'm an environmentalist. I wouldn't harm an endangered species."

"You mean we've made the list?"

"There are more of us than you, and we have to take care of those who are left around. It's simple mathematics. Without your kind, there's none of us, and where would the world be then? That's a very important reason why we're opposed to war. They take only the healthy and intelligent to fight. We need all our healthy and intelligent men to produce healthy and intelligent female babies to protect the world from men."

"Uh..."

"Never mind. You needn't bother your pretty head about it, male sperm bank. We'll figure it all out for you and just tell you where to be, when."

"I believe things are getting out of hand. We're losing control."

"In the nick of time."

"My trouble is, I almost agree with you."

"That you should be a sperm bank?"

"That women would do a better job of it."

"Is that taped?" she called out elaborately.

"Trapped. I thought it was perfectly safe to say that, under these circumstances, in order to pander to your female ego. Actually, we need women for only one reason: cooking and cleaning, and hanky-panky."

"That's three reasons. And you forgot doing the laundry at the creek."

"See? You know your place."

She shrieked and attacked, and they rolled around and played. He pinned her again. When he lay spent and complaining about being used up, she stood up and put her bare foot on his bare stomach and gave the Tarzan yell. She leaned over and said, "Tate would be proud of me. She never let us use the yell, so she didn't know I practiced in private. That was pretty good, wasn't it?"

"It was super— Oh, you mean the yell. Naw, it goes this way." And he did a bull bellow that rattled the windows.

She stood there, looking astonished, and said, "I suspected you were a bull all along. Here I thought I had you helpless, and you can still do *that*? I . . . suppose . . . I'll have to . . . do it . . . again."

And she sat down on him, as he begged, "No. No. Not again. Help. Help help help." But he arranged her to suit himself and her eyes flew open, and she shrieked and got off him and ran to her room, opened the magic door and closed it after her.

He lay on his side on one elbow, his head propped on a hand, laughing, his eyes glinting, and he knew he was going to have to get past that door soon now. It was her retreat of last resort and she thought she was impregnable.

They grocery-shopped that afternoon. Instead of four miles, they ran only two around the jogging trail, and they didn't say much. They were companionable. They got their laundry done, and they were together. But she still treated him more as a friend than as the lover he wanted her to recognize.

She said, "Under odd circumstances, I've noticed that although you're blond on your head, the other hair on you is darker, like your eyebrows. Why is that? Do you bleach your hair?"

He was superior. "No. My dad's hair was this way, and one of my brothers is, too. We're like this all our lives. The hair on our bodies darken if we're not in the sun, and the hair on our heads gets yellower, but it stays blond. If I'm out in the sun all the time, it gets white on top."

"I love the combination of blond hair and dark eyebrows."

He was elated. That was a giant step up from the fact that she'd allowed him to share her place because she'd never cared for blonds. Did she care enough? "Let's get married."

She pulled back a little, she was so amazed, and she stared at him with a little frown.

He was disgruntled. "I've mentioned it. You shouldn't be that surprised."

"I just can't see how you think we should do something so serious that fast."

"Don't you think making love is serious?"

She considered his mood. It was he who was serious. She smiled slowly before she said "Well, it's certainly fun!" She grinned at him. "I'm so glad you came along when you did. I might never have known anything but what difficult apartmentmates women can be. I hear there are some who are great, but I haven't yet found one. I've had five, counting those in college. And they've all been a pain. You're marvelous."

"If you'd had another man instead of me, would you have made love with him?"

"How could I know?"

"I think it was just a good thing I was the first one who came along. You're a wild woman—you were a fire waiting to be lit. I was lucky. But I can't have you going around tasting any other man. So you need to marry me and be committed."

To soften her words, she stretched up and kissed his mouth. "You have to know how involved I am with the environment. I need time to do my share. I worry about the world."

"You can worry about the world, married to me, as easily as you can do it on your own."

"I'm not sure...that I would want to bring children into the world, as it is today."

"Don't be such a coward. There have been times of stress and fear all during time. And people were brave enough to live, and love and help. We can do no less. Whether or not we have children doesn't matter as much as our being together. But I would like to have some kids."

"Don't spoil this time by crowding me. I do like you. But I have my own life."

"You have some corners to share with me."

"You give me all that talk about believing women would do a better job of it. That I have 'corners' to share, and I could go on and live any way I want, and all that. And it sounds good. But Graham, you are a dominant male if ever I saw one, and being a Texan, I was raised on them. I recognize your type. I know what you will do. You'll give me a whole song and dance about being liberal, and you mean every word, but it's all talk. If some other woman got away with it, you'd be tolerant, but you'd expect me to be the classically submissive female."

He'd nodded his head in little, contemplative bounces, all through her dissertation, and when she was through, he agreed. "That's just about it."

She *had* expected him to give more lip service, and when he out-and-out *admitted* being just that way, she put her hands in her hair and shrieked.

A little crossly impatient, he warned her "You've got to quit making all those shrieking noises. The neighbors haven't come to inquire yet, but they must be getting curious. That Tarzan yell alone must have raised the hair on their heads. But they *will* get around to investigating. And one of these times I'm going to have to explain your attitude to strangers, and that won't be easy."

"I should have run a better check on you."

He smiled benignly. "Everybody loves me."

"And you? Do you love everybody? How many women have you lived with?"

And giving tit for tat, so to speak, he replied loftily, "You're my first."

She hadn't expected just that reply and it made her a little thoughtful.

So it was during that week, as he struggled with an overload of cases and a couple of late nights, when they really didn't see each other because she was back in her own room, that he heard it again. It was during lunch with his varying collection of regulars when one of the women said of her husband, "He was so sweet. I was sick as a horse and couldn't really appreciate him at first. I was hoping I'd die, but I did get over that idea, and then I began to notice how worried he was, and I was so touched. He's been really sweet to me. I don't think he ever realized how much he'd miss me."

Her friend began, "Isn't it awful that it takes something like—"

But Graham had quit listening. That was what Roberta needed. She needed to realize he was precious to her. He needed to get sick.

Nine

So Graham tried to get sick. He'd been so healthy all his life that he'd never taken any conscious preventative measures to avoid illness. Of course, he washed his hands just through habit, he ate well, and he exercised because it felt good. So it seemed to him that the opposite could do the trick and he'd get sick.

He pictured himself lying in bed, and Roberta hovering over him. He'd chill, and she'd strip off her clothes and get into bed with him, her cool flesh feeling good to his fevered body. He smiled as he drove along home, feeling her against his hot body, just like always. Umm, if his body was chilling, would his flesh be hot?

He worked on that. It would be logical that if he was chilling, she would be warm to him. But she was so cool and he was always so blazing hot, that his fantasy kept that sequence as he imagined what all would happen when she tried to warm him. He smiled some more.

So he ate junk food, he didn't run, and he stood in the way of other people who coughed. He went without his coat and hat, and he stood in drafts. He stayed healthy. He felt stuffy and dull, but he stayed well. No colds, no complaints. All he needed was some fresh air.

Flu hit the entire area, and the work force was decimated, but Graham stayed well. He hated to think of Roberta getting sick, and watched her with some divided feelings. If she got sick, he could take care of her. That would work a lot better, because he could easily dream of his hot body toasting her cold and chilling one. And he could dream about accepting her gratitude.

But he didn't like the idea of her not feeling well. So he was careful of her. He washed his hands and he coaxed her to take vitamins and drink lots of water and fruit juices. She stayed well, and he did feel a twinge of disappointment, but *he* stayed well, and he could only be disgusted.

He said to a friend, "If I could get sick, maybe my roommate would take care of me and fall madly in love with me. But I'm never sick." And he frowned, disgruntled.

His friend gave Graham a patient look and said, "Fake it."

Well, of course! Why hadn't such a simple solution occurred to him? Because basically he was an honest man. She would never appreciate the strain it would put on his character, or his good opinion of himself, for him to lie about his health. But, he thought, all's fair in love and war.

He was lying on the sofa with a quilt over him and a cloth on his forehead when she came in that night after a fund-raiser. She banged back the door and stood over him. "I just met a friend of yours," she snarled down at him.

Interest rising, he said, "Oh?"

"Does 'Sharon' ring a bell?" And, not waiting for a reply, she whirled away and stormed around the partition into the kitchen, and he heard her door open and close again, permanently.

He sat there in pure disgust. So much for languishing and garnering any concern today. He got up and put away the cloth and the quilt. He went out and jogged in desperation. And he didn't see her for two days.

The next time they met, she came in and he was lying on the sofa watching a murder take place on TV. She stood and looked down at him in a hostile way. He smiled wanly and held his head, as he rose to his feet. "You'd better not kiss me," he warned. "I think I'm coming down with something." Of course, she hadn't *offered* to kiss him, but it seemed a good way not only to point that out to her, but to introduce the subject of his fragile health.

She reached up and felt his forehead. "No fever." She turned on the light. "Sit down." She angled his head and said, "Open your mouth and say 'Ah.' You're fine." And she went to her sanctuary, leaving him there to die of irritated embarrassment. She ought to have figured out he needed some attention.

The flu waned and the first victims came back pale and weak. He looked at them all with black envy. He continued hale and hearty.

She avoided him. So the next night he waited up for her to come home, stalk by him in her continuing snit, and he took her arm and asked, "Do you want me to move out?"

She stopped in astonishment. "Why?"

"You haven't really spoken to me in days. I thought it might be better if I just leave."

With irritation she asked, "Just because I'm mad at you for being so cozy with that woman, you think you ought to move out? Great. What a marvelous mentality you have. You don't know from beans!" And she stormed off again.

He stood blinking and trying to puzzle that all out but found it too confusing. Apparently she didn't want him to leave. If she didn't want that, then it seemed logical to figure that she wanted him to make up with her. He smiled. He walked with an authoritative stride over to her door and put his hand on the magic portal and turned the knob. It was locked.

He couldn't believe that. He rattled the doorknob and slapped his big, hard hand on the panel and said, "Roberta! Open this door."

And just on the other side of the door, she shouted back, "Go away, you womanizer!"

"Look, Roberta, I didn't actually sleep with her. It was just, well, it just happened. It wasn't like... with us."

"I was easier!"

"No, you weren't. Honey, let me—"

"Get away from my door."

He really seriously considered lifting his foot and fixing that lock, but she was just on the other side and she could be hurt. So he walked back across the kitchen, making the floor rattle a little with his hard heels, and went into the living room to fling himself down on the sofa.

Her door opened, and she went into the kitchen to bang pans around. He got up and stood at the end of the partition so that he could see her. She ignored him rather elaborately. He took two long steps over, scooped her against him and kissed her silly.

She struggled inadequately, then finally gave up to endure it. But her hands went to his shoulders, and her body relaxed—it was so tired. She was just going to wait until he realized—but his tongue licked along and poked a little at her lips, and her mouth gave up. It was then she realized he was holding her off the floor all by himself, so she put her arms around his shoulders, and after that she was just a spectator.

He carried her helpless body into his room, put it on his bed and did all sorts of things to it, and he . . . used it. She was simply overwhelmed, and she couldn't prevent it at all, at all. It was useless to struggle, and she shivered with her climax. A little smile came unbidden, and he saw it when she smiled the second time.

He smiled back. "You've put me through one hell of a wringer. You ought to be sent to bed without your supper for acting so mean and ornery."

"I wasn't the one who fooled around with a no-good somebody."

"Sharon's a nice woman. You're the hellcat. Are you going to say you're sorry for being so mean to me lately?"

"After you."

"I'm sorry I met Sharon six months before I knew you existed, and that I was almost attracted to her. But at that time, I didn't know you were alive."

"I waited for you."

"Umm, Roberta, I love you. Marry me."

"Now we're back to that. I've already told you all about how I feel about that."

"But you were jealous. You love me."

"No, it's just a matter of loyalty."

"Honey, be reasonable. How could I be loyal to you if I didn't even know you?"

"I'll think of a reason in a minute or two. I've missed you."

"I've been here all the time."

"Did you really feel ill that night I came home and you were on the sofa?"

"What night was that?" He was rash.

She struggled from him and snapped, "When I'd just met Sharon. She said—" Roberta made her voice drip with sweetness "—'I hear you're living with Graham Rawlins, you lucky girl, you.'"

His curiosity ran rampant. "What did you say to that?"

"I told her kindly that I was a 'woman.'"

Graham nodded. She would have, there was no question of that.

"She said, 'If you weren't one when he moved in, you'd be one now.'"

She'd remembered that conversation all this time, so he had to mean something to her. He put his hand on the back of her head and leaned his head down closer to her. "You love me."

"No, I respect you as a person, and I won't have some bitch bandying your name about that way."

"You care about me."

"I am loyal to a co-resident."

"You were jealous."

"Yes."

The admission was thrilling to him and he had to part his lips to take a quick breath. He held her closely, relishing the meager admission that she cared about him.

After that night they both became really busy. He turned his thoughts particularly to his job overload. He went back to his regular diet, and health regimen; and he jogged again, glad to be alive, and feeling sorry for the surviving flu victims, who were gradually returning to work. He was being especially careful of Roberta. She was so fragile that flu would really knock her out. She worked too hard. He cosseted her.

They both traveled in that time for their various responsibilities. When they met, it was as people who've been alone in the sea and who've both swum to the same spar, to find a fellow survivor. Their love making wasn't the leisurely play it had been. It was renewal, a period of relief, an oasis in their hectic schedule. And it was love of another kind.

Roberta actually was home before Graham one night, and he only had time to open the door when she said, "Georgina is going to actually *marry* that strange man! I'm going down next weekend for the wedding. Would you like to go along?"

See? There she was, treating him like a fond acquaintance. He said, "I would be delighted."

"I'm glad. I would like your opinion of Finnig. His first name is Quintus. Apparently he was a gambler. God only knows what else. Daddy adroitly avoids giving an opinion of him. And mother says, in her way, 'He's different and so interesting.' But I would like you to tell me what you think of him—as a man. I think you 'see' people clearly and judge them quite well.

You'll love my sisters. Everyone will be there, and you'll get to see them all. My parents are perfect. If you don't believe they are, keep your opinion of them to yourself."

He laughed and hugged her. "Tell me about them."

"I already did. They are perfect."

"I shall look forward to approving of them."

She grinned, then she widened her eyes. "The blue-bonnets will be in bloom! Oh, Graham, you are in for a treat. Speaking of treats, I won't get to sleep with you there."

"I understand. Mother's the same way." But he was distracted because she implied that she considered him a "treat." She loved him. If only she would admit it.

"I have to be in Utah on Monday." She turned her head and looked at him. "Will you notice that I'm not here?"

He couldn't treat the question frivolously. "I'll miss you terribly."

"Oh, Graham, you are sweet."

"I love you."

"Now don't start that again."

He kissed her, and she responded with fervor, and he began to believe she would finally admit that she loved him.

But then she said, "It's just a good thing that George chose this weekend, because I'll be gone for two weeks, and I could never leave Utah for just a wedding. It would take something much more serious than that."

He looked at her soberly. She didn't consider a sister's wedding ceremony serious enough for her inconvenience or striving? She was only going to this one because it was handy to do so? Was she so imbued with the carelessness to commitment that she allowed a wedding to take on such casual overtones? She shocked him to his farm-bred toes. And that wiped out all the little bits and pieces of her comments that he'd treasured as indicative of her regard. He lost heart.

He changed. Roberta felt it, and as they flew to Texas that Thursday night, she looked at him frequently. "Are you feeling well?"

His melancholy of despair had left him sublevel in awareness and he asked courteously, "What?"

"Are you okay?"

"Fine."

But she frowned at him.

He continued subdued. They landed in San Antonio and took a small plane to Kerrville, where Georgina and Quint met them. George was exuberant and laughing and glad to see them. Quint watched George as if she was the key to life and he couldn't lose sight of her. Graham shook hands with a fellowman whom he understood.

As Roberta had predicted, Graham loved all her sisters, and her parents were obviously perfect. So was their house. He stood in front of it and looked at that big house with its wraparound porches. The family dogs had intelligent eyes and watched everyone in a way that was level and quiet.

The people went up onto the porch, then on inside, all that noisy, laughing bunch. Graham saw the lovely house interior, and the carefully chosen, casually treated treasures that suited them all. He noted that the family cats were used to people and noise and found guests interesting. Then he saw the bird cage that was two stories tall, and he understood them all a little more.

His regret was that he had relinquished ever belonging in this crowd of special people. George loved Quint; there was no question of that. As Hillary loved Angus, and Tate loved Bill. Roberta's sisters were different, one from the other, but their love for their husbands was clear, as was that of the parents'. All that love, given in different ways and at different levels; all that liking. But Roberta didn't have that ability.

She enjoyed sex. She made a good friend. But the commitment of love was beyond her. She'd just brought him along as a friend, as a companion. That was all he could expect from her. And Graham grieved. Jim had been right to escape. Jim had realized that Roberta was incapable of loving him. She hadn't even remembered having met Jim before he came to see Graham.

Graham knew that Roberta would remember him. He had been her first lover, and it was said that women always had a fond memory of a first lover. What a sad commentary on the times. He'd been her first, and she'd probably written him into a diary as such, therefore she would remember him.

"Are you okay?" Roberta questioned him. "You're not getting the flu, are you? I would hate for us to bring that bug down here."

"I'm okay."

"You acted this way about Jim. Have you heard from him? I thought your quarrel was settled."

"Jim? No. I've heard from him. He's glad he's in England. He's settled in well. There's never been a quarrel with him per se. I'll tell you about that some day. Perhaps later this month. I'm thinking of transferring away from D.C." He looked around the Lambert house. "I believe I'd like to go to a smaller place and set up practice." He smiled rather sadly. "I think I'll buy this house from your parents and move it by helicopter to wherever I am."

"You're leaving D.C.?"

"I would like to marry you and live happily ever after, but you don't want that. So I need to move on. You'll be better off without me. I would only nag at you. We'd end up quarreling, and it would be very miserable for you. This way would be better."

"Who would I live with?"

And to Graham that was the coup de grace, the final, killing blow. She thought only of who would be her next co-resident. She gave no thought to losing him.

During the day of preparation for the wedding party, there was the bustle of the cooks, hired help, deliveries, and chatting. There was the laughter and movement, but to Graham, the courtesy of the Lamberts and their guests was all rather vague to him.

Roberta drove Graham down the road to meet her grandparents, and she took him out into the fields of bluebonnets. She picked one and allowed him to hold it and smell its pungent fragrance. It was meaningless to him. He was withholding his emotions in self-protection. She held his hand, but it only tore his heart because she was inherently kind, and she was killing him gently.

On Friday night was the groom's dinner, which they all attended. Afterward, they returned to the Lambert house, and Roberta coaxed Graham to play the piano. Like everything else in their home, the piano was exceptional—a beautiful instrument and perfectly tuned. One note thrilled his soul, and he sat down with some anticipation of pleasure.

Everyone else settled in a wary way, and Roberta laughed softly for their coming surprise. They were treated to a superb concert of three pieces. Still hungry for Graham's music, they protested but he said, "No more, now."

George asked, "Play for me tomorrow. Play when I come down the stairs to Quint. Play 'Oh Promise Me,' please."

He smiled gently at the bride-to-be and replied, "I'd be honored."

The others applauded, and Roberta leaned against Graham's arm and smiled up at him.

Gradually people went to bed, but Graham had been told to linger. So the husbands and Graham had a nightcap with the groom in the two-story solarium, which adjoined the bird cage.

The four men were all cordial. Only Fredricka, the second-eldest daughter, was not represented by a male.

Graham wished he could go to bed. He'd been strained to match the festive feeling, and he was tired.

The men spoke to Quint of being married to a Lambert. It was easy banter. Graham gradually realized that Bill and Angus were almost unknowingly fond of Quintus. They didn't understand him, but they were loyal to him. And there was an odd respect. Even grudging admiration.

Quint didn't care whether he was liked or not, but he was willing to be cordial. He loved Georgina. He spoke carefully, in a rather stilted way, and his comments were brief. Their drinks were almost consumed when Quint said to Graham, "It won't be easy."

That didn't make sense, so Graham looked at Quint with a slight, puzzled frown. And the other two men became alert and were silent.

Quint said, "I tried not to love Georgina." He was the only one who called George by her proper name.

Graham listened, and the other two smiled and exchanged a glance.

Quint went on. "I did my damndest to leave her alone. To stay away from her. It didn't work. It won't for you, either."

Graham looked into Quint's similar eyes and understood that Quint had recognized Graham's dilemma. He told his surprise advocate, "She has no interest in me at all. There's no hope."

But Quint countered, "She cares about you."

"She refuses to marry me."

The three men smiled and shifted in their chairs and exchanged laughing glances. The other two said versions of "The Lambert women are different. You have to be patient. Don't do anything rash."

But it was Quint who said "Don't give her any choices. Stick to convincing her."

Graham was very touched by their support. But *their* Lambert daughters were different from the one he'd drawn. To go the route they approved would be futile. He pointed out, "Roberta is an environmentalist. She thinks marriage would be distracting, and she doesn't want to bring children into this world, the way it is."

Tate's Bill asked, "Have you watched her with Tate's son, Benjamin? Have you listened to her talk to my Jenny? Have you watched her with Tate, who is pregnant?"

Hillary's Angus elaborated, "Roberta is giving you a smoke screen. She just needs convincing."

And Quint cautioned, "Don't louse up."

Graham nodded once to indicate he'd heard, and he smiled a glance at each to thank them for their advice. They did mean well.

Quint said, "If we can get Fredricka married, we'll have a poker club."

Bill replied to that: "Play poker with you? I'll bet you invented the game."

Quint nodded sagely and told Graham, "The pros always start that way. They try to make you think they don't know nothing, but you will note that he said, 'I'll bet.' He is a man who takes chances. He'd be a hell of an opponent."

Angus corroborated that. "Bill's a formidable bridge player. He's probably equally adept at poker."

Bill lifted his chin and frowned. "How many do you meld in poker?"

And the other men laughed. They talked a while longer, then they said good-night and went off to their beds.

Graham lay awake for a while. He not only regretted his lack of success with Roberta, but he would miss knowing those three men. And realizing it was hopeless, he waited to see if Roberta would come to him. But she did not.

She came to his room in the morning and knocked, then opened the door and came in quite sassily. He was lying on his stomach, and he opened his tired eyes to watch his love, feeling closer to Jim then he'd ever imagined.

Roberta came to the bed saying, "You lazy bum. Do you think there's no payment for your bed and board? We have errands—" She reached and pulled off the covers and lifted a hand to smack his bottom...and he was naked.

Even he had to smile, she looked so surprised.

He turned over slowly, and she gasped. He held out a hand invitingly, but she covered her face and laughed. "You wicked, *wicked* man to tempt me this way!"

"*Are* you tempted? How can I seal you to me? How can I convince you that you love me?"

She sobered and frowned at him. Then she turned away and walked a step or two before she looked back at him, lying there so beautifully naked. She said, "We need to run some errands. Do you want to come along?"

"All right."

"Breakfast is ready downstairs. I'll...go on down." Her troubled eyes stayed on him.

"I'll be down in a minute."

"All right."

And she left him there.

During the day, Graham did his full share of work, and Roberta thanked him for agreeing to play for George's wedding.

Being a piano player, he knew all about background music. He loved playing, and to play on the Lambert's instrument was such a pleasure, he didn't mind at all.

The house slowly filled with people, and Graham took his place early at the piano. He was interrupted by Roberta, who found people he had to meet. He didn't mind that, either. There were those who came and leaned on the piano and watched but who also listened and nodded to him. He was very skilled.

When George came down with her covey of sisters in their various gowns so beautiful, so charming, such a picture, he played "Oh Promise Me" with great emotion, and there was silence.

Afterward, in the crush of the reception, George came and sat beside him and kissed his cheek. "You made it complete."

And during that time, as he continued to play, Roberta came and sat beside him. He finished the piece, then turned and looked at her.

She studied him, then reached to put her hand on his forehead. "Are you feeling all right?"

He began to play again. "I'm fine."

"Are you tired of playing? If you'd like to stop, we understand. I didn't bring you here to entertain."

"I love to play."

"There are people who would like to talk to you who hate to interrupt."

He finished the piece and turned. "Okay."

And everyone he met thanked him for his beautiful music. Some grieved that they could not play an instrument. Some envied him the ability. Some said they could play but nobody ever invited *them* to play on that piano. And there were a couple of guests who quarreled as to who got to play next. And they did play.

George whispered, "Have I mentioned that I'm glad it was you who played?"

As all the family complimented him and saw to it that he met people and treated him as one of them, he regretted even more that Roberta couldn't love him...enough. For she did care about him. She stayed with him, introduced him with pride and bragged on him, while she held his hand. And Bill or Quint or Angus would catch Graham's glance to grin or nod encouragement or wink or give him a discreet, finger-curled-to thumb sign. It was like family. It was very nice to be included as one of them so easily. Roberta did care. But not enough.

After brunch Quint and George were saying good-bye before leaving on their honeymoon. Her daddy asked very puzzled, ''Why would you want to go anywhere but Texas? I suppose it's because you need to give that woman some attention, and if you stayed here for the honeymoon, the beautiful state would distract you?'' As is typical of Southerners, he questioned with statement, thereby asking agreement.

Quint said, ''Right.'' And he said, ''Thank you for all the trouble.'' And he said, ''I'll take good care of Georgina.''

Her dad smiled and patted Quint's shoulder, then hugged the big man.

It was another noisy time, and Graham watched and listened. He became homesick. Home. He needed to see his own family, especially his mother.

Roberta was as involved in the farewells as all the rest of her family, but she courteously stayed by Graham's side and held his hand.

After the newlyweds drove off, the party continued. Everyone was saying, ''Well, that leaves only two Lambert daughters loose. We've had two great parties this year, but that's enough for now. Roberta, Fredricka, don't get married right away. We need some space in between these shindigs so we'll appreciate them more. Too close together, and the parties will become ordinary.''

Someone exclaimed, ''A Lambert gathering ordinary?''

That incredulous questioning brought laughter, and they all went back inside to linger and talk and eat and drink for the rest of the day. There were good people there—old friends that money can't buy. They were loving, friendly, easy people. And Graham was homesick for his own family.

Or was his longing for his family a primitive retreat from hurt? He needed his own people around him, because after Roberta's rejection of him, then he could know himself as valued. And with that family support, he could begin to heal. He grieved again that his father was no longer with them. He needed his dad's counsel. He would go home the next day. He would see his relatives for a few hours before he returned to D.C. When he got back, he would see about reordering his life.

Ten

That night when the house was silent, Graham was still dressed and standing at his window, looking out over the moonlit yard. The door to his room silently opened, and Roberta came into his room. She raised her finger to her lips to hush him, as she soundlessly closed his door.

She smiled as naughtily as a child who has sneaked downstairs late on Christmas eve and is preparing to open gifts.

Did she consider him a gift? One that could be opened and used and forgotten? Jim had misread her. He'd said she needed to marry a man who could love her and give her children. She didn't want either. This lovely temptress was a hollow woman.

She came toward him, utterly charming, so delightful. She was teasing and beautiful; exactly what every man wanted in a woman. Except Graham. He wanted

more, but she didn't. She had no need for commitment. He could take her and play her game for as long
as it pleased her; but after that, he would be abandoned. He'd realized this, but he felt enough self-
preservation that he now chose not to play. He held her
and he kissed her, but it was in goodbye.

He said, "I can't make covert love to you here. And
I must get to bed. I'm catching the predawn flight to
Indiana. Since I'm traveling, I thought I'd go back
through Fort Wayne and see my folks. I know you're
going to be gone for a while. I'll call you in Utah if
anything comes up. You'll leave a number at the office?"

"You're going to see your family? When did you
decide to do that?"

"It's been a while since I've been home. Maybe it
was seeing your people. You have a great family. You
are really fond of each other, and perhaps it made me
homesick. Thank you for asking me to come along.
I've enjoyed it. Good luck. Out in Utah."

She was watching him, very alert. "What time do
you leave the house in the morning?"

"Six. Bill's taking me."

"I'll be seeing you." She stood on tiptoe and kissed
his chin.

His voice roughened, he said, "Goodbye."

She turned back at the door and waggled her fingers
at him, then she was gone. Forever. It would be his last
glimpse of her.

But it wasn't. In the morning, she was dressed and
packed, drinking coffee and saying to him, "If you
don't get a move on it, Graham Rawlins, we're going
to be late."

And Bill had the audacity to comment privately to Graham, "Tried to get away, did you? The Lambert sisters never allow anything so stupid to happen. Relax." Then, because he was a fisherman, he added, "Let her reel you in."

That only showed what little Bill knew of the situation.

Graham and Roberta flew in to Chicago and had good connections to Fort Wayne, where Graham's next-older brother met him. They hugged and laughed, needing no words. But his brother was excessively conscious of Roberta. It was very awkward for Graham. It wasn't awkward for Roberta, who fit in instantly, curious, friendly and interested. Graham could have throttled her.

He found time to explain to his mother that Roberta was not there to be judged. She wasn't interested. He had asked her to marry him, but she'd turned him down. And he said he was thinking of moving back west. His plans weren't solid, but he would have some idea in the next two weeks.

His mother saw that although Graham didn't touch Roberta, she would look at him to check his reaction to her comments. And Roberta touched Graham. She sat next to him, and she was charming to his family.

But Mrs. Rawlins saw the pain in her son's eyes, and her protective maternal instincts came, unbidden. She was cool to the young woman who was torturing her son. Her courtesy was there, but she was a little formal with Roberta. The others picked up on that and knew something was wrong.

They were especially tender to Graham. Several carloads of people went to the airport to tell them goodbye. And they were soon en route to Dayton to change planes for D.C.

"Why was your mother disapproving of me? Did you tell her we're sleeping together?"

"I told her I'd asked you to marry me but you refused. She was excited when I brought you home. She thought it was an announcement. I couldn't let her hope."

"So that was it. I knew I'd done something wrong. She's a stern woman. She loves you."

"She has to, she's my mother."

"I've seen mothers who didn't like their children."

"I wonder how you would have been with children."

"I'm going to save the world for children. Everybody's children."

Graham saw that her jaw was set and her eyes sparkled with more than determination.

There wasn't any way that he could deny himself that night, and he made love to her. It was exquisite agony, for it was the last time. Another goodbye. He held her to him against his hungry body, and he suffered dreadful grief for his love. He began to really understand all the ramifications of love, and he finally really understood Jim.

Roberta was a slowly curling delight of seduction. She teased and tempted and allowed him to taste the fruits of paradise. She touched and pleasured and kissed as she lured him to his destruction. For without her, he would never again be whole. When he left her, when he escaped from her, he would leave a part of himself. It was being torn from him in this joining.

Was it his soul that he would leave with her? Would he be forever soulless in his wanderings now? How could his body survive without it? How could he survive without her?

He told her, "I love you."

"You know I must leave in the morning. I'll be gone for two weeks. Will you miss me?"

"I'll miss you all of my life."

"It's only for two weeks." She kissed him marvelously. She embraced him and petted him. She murmured how he pleased her, and she ruffled his hair and said, "I never did like blonds." And she laughed, holding him to her.

Her body was familiar to him. He knew where she liked to be touched. He touched her and watched her reaction carefully so that he could dream it correctly. He watched his hands on her and registered how she looked and how she moved so that he could remember exactly.

And he kissed her with all the emotion of his being, with all of his love. And when he moved into her sheath, he did it carefully so that he would recall perfectly how it felt to him, how her arms enclosed him, how she slid the soles of her feet to the backs of his legs and rubbed them there.

When he moved, he did it for memory. He did it for her response, and for all the feelings in his body, of his own to treasure. He loved her. He loved her more than his life. And he could not get enough of her in this final meeting, this final melding of their bodies.

The night was over, too soon. The alarm went off, and she jumped up. Then she came back and kissed him very hard. "Take care of yourself."

And she was gone.

* * *

He showered and dressed on automatic. Most of him
was rather impressed that he could function so well. He
listened to himself at the office and was pleased with
this other, automatic self who could manage without
him. Since that was being done, he could decide what
he was really going to do about his life. He was going
to get rid of the headache first. By George, he really
had a terrible headache. He mentioned it to his other
self, who efficiently got him two aspirins.

While this other self dispatched an endless amount
of work, he lolled back inside himself and concocted
various schemes and plans. None was satisfactory. This
was going to take some time.

After a seeming year of time, the day was finally
completed. He could only trust to the god of all distracted people that his work was satisfactory. He went
home to that empty apartment, to his empty life. He
drank two glasses of water with three aspirins, and he
went to bed.

That, he realized, was different. But he'd had a hard
weekend. And he'd spent the night before making love
to Roberta. The end. The end. The end. He really
didn't feel very well.

Wouldn't it be weird if he got sick *now* when it
wouldn't do him any good at all? Roberta was gone for
two weeks. He'd be well by the time she got home
again. Damn. With his luck, that's what would happen.

He got up in the middle of the next morning, called
in sick, ate some soup and went back to bed. His lousy
luck was holding. He was really sick. He surfaced once
to go to the bathroom and get some water. Then he
went to the kitchen, got a pitcher and put it by his bed.

After that, he lost count of everything. He did remember getting up on occasion, but a couple a very blank days passed.

He remembered chills. And he remembered finding himself at Roberta's bedroom door, and discovering it open, he couldn't bring himself to go through it to her. He burst out laughing, and he laughed over whatever it was that was so funny all the way back to his rumpled, freezing bed.

Then some strange man was sitting next to him, patting his face, not very gently, and asking him, "What's your name?"

His eyes focused on the stranger and Graham licked dry lips before he asked, "Who the hell are you?"

"I'm a doctor. I was here this morning, don't you remember? I gave you one hell of a shot, and you seemed to notice that."

"Leave me alone."

"I've probably saved your worthless life. I should have given you strychnine. How could you have gotten Roberta in just a couple of weeks? I turn my back and she's hooked by some yahoo I've never seen before. Here you are, moved in and in control."

"'In control'?" Graham was baffled. "In control of...what?"

"Roberta. She called me this morning, hysterical. I had to get Maintenance. Then we both had to wrestle you. Hold still, damn it."

"You've already done that! Get away! Leave me alone!"

"With pleasure. She'll be here in another couple of hours. You're going to make it."

All that wove itself into strange dreams. He opened his eyes once and something was on his chest. A creature all eyes and hair. He hollered and swung, and it disappeared.

Then she came. She came all soft and sweet and put her cool hand on his head. Then she lay on his chest, and he couldn't breathe.

He felt something poked in the corner of his mouth, and her voice said, "It's a straw. Drink." And cool water came into his mouth. Then it was soup. Then it was liquid Jell-O.

But big hands seized him as someone turned him ungently and made his move, and it irritated him. A harsh voice called, "Roberta! Come help." That wasn't his voice. Who was there? But his hearing was strange and maybe he *was* calling to her. Then her voice soothed him, murmuring, and he quieted.

In the weird replay of nightmares, that nasty man was back and gave Graham another shot. Again they exchanged harsh words, but this time there was the soothing murmur of Roberta's remembered voice. And he slept.

Feeling at peace, he opened his eyes. He felt suspended in time. All was well. He breathed...and could. That was nice. He felt clean and sleepy. And he went to sleep.

When he wakened again, it was to the precious dream of her hand. He opened his eyes, and it was true. Roberta was there, and her hand was on his forehead. He stared. And she smiled as if it wasn't a miracle.

"Roberta?" his voice croaked.

"Are you lucid?" She petted his scratchy cheek. "You're still pretty hot."

"Are you a dream?"

"An abused nurse a dream?"

"I hurt you?"

"No, of course not. But you sure gave poor Ralph a hard time."

In his mind Graham considered a mean voice. "Was he the one who stuck me?"

"No, that was Robin."

"A bird?" He wasn't really in touch, and she confused him.

"A doctor. He's an internist and lives in the complex. Or he has until now. With all the trouble you've given him, he'll probably move."

"How—?"

"I called him. I'd called you, and you babbled. I couldn't make any sense, and I knew you weren't drunk. So I called Robin, and then I flew home."

"I'm more important than a wedding?"

"What wedding?"

"You said George was lucky she was being married before you went to Utah, or you wouldn't have made the wedding."

Roberta—the cool, the organized, the distanced woman—blushed scarlet and looked aside. But then she looked back at Graham and admitted, "Yes."

He was awed. He concentrated and reached for clarification. "I'm right up there with the environment?"

"You're an endangered species. I told you that."

"Why are you preserving me?"

She took a steadying breath and told him, "Out in Utah, I realized that there have to be concerned citizens all through the future. I won't be around forever, and I should have children. There must be others to carry the torch, so to speak. So I've changed my mind, and if you haven't already found someone else to marry, I'd like you to reconsider me."

He was a little fuzzy, sorting out her words and meaning. "You want me as a sperm bank?"

"Among other things."

"When . . . exactly . . . did you change your mind?"

She'd been rather self-consciously sassy up until then, but now she sobered and just looked at him. "When I realized you were very sick, I panicked. I was so far from you, and there was no one to help you. You needed me. You're so big and strong and self-determined. You do everything so fantasically effortlessly. How does a woman help a man like that? But you needed me. I called Robin. The flu epidemic is so bad, there isn't any room in the hospitals. They locked your outer door and checked on you hourly. I got here as soon as I could. I'll probably be fired. I drove your car."

The fact that she'd driven his car did catch a fragment of his attention. She had tacked it on the end of her words so strangely, and he filed the information away. He decided that before they went any further with this discussion, she ought to know. "Robin loves you. I distinctly remember him telling me that I'd muscled my way into your life."

"You silly." She laughed that deliciously gentle sound his ears loved. "While you were delirious you told me that, and you told me Jim what's-his-name left the country because of me." She smiled down at him in an "I'm more mature than you but I love you and can tolerate your little foibles" kind of gentleness. "I only saw Jim that once."

"You don't remember *Jim*?"

Patiently she reminded Graham, "He was here at our party."

"He was here with some papers, and you saw him before you met me." He frowned, trying to concentrate.

"Why...that's right. Well, it doesn't matter at all. Let me get you some water. Here, sip this. Good. Now, sleep. Go to sleep, darling. We'll talk later."

He slept uneasily. He needed to be alert to defend Roberta against marauding abductors. Then it settled into his subconscious: she would marry him in order to have children to cope with the pollution of the future. She *would* marry him. And he was sad. He wanted her to love him beyond even the environment.

When he wakened again, she wasn't there, and he figured he'd dreamed her, having manufactured her apparition from his imagination. But he was conscious of how comfortable he was. He lay there and scratched his face. His beard was growing. He felt it with knowledgeable fingers. When had he decided to grow a beard? It was ten o'clock. What day? Must be Saturday? He pushed back the covers and sat up. He felt strange.

He heard a sound, and she came into his room. He stared.

She smiled and said, "Are you strong enough to get up?"

She was in Utah. He felt as drained as if he'd made continuous love for two weeks. "Roberta." He was confused, so he just said her name to see what she'd reply.

She asked, "What's your name?"

He knew that's what they asked football players on the field who've been hit hard. Had he been in a

wreck? He felt like it. "What's going on? Why aren't
you in Utah?" He stood up and was surprised that he
was unsteady. Only then did he realize he must have
been sick.

"I came home." The simple reply should tell him
everything.

"Why?"

"To take care of you." She came to him and stood
looking up at him with such tender eyes.

"You ought to keep your distance. I must have really
been sick."

"Sit down."

He did, rather abruptly.

She lifted his legs into the bed and re-covered him.
"You mustn't hurry it. It'll take a while for you to get
well. This is a wicked bug. Are you hungry?"

His head was oddly light. It felt as if it wasn't actually attached to his body. "I don't know. You said
you drove my car?"

"Yes."

"Why?"

"To get some aspirin and to grocery-shop." She'd
tell him the rest when he was stronger.

"That's okay."

"You're a rotten patient. You were rude to Ralph
and Robin."

"To you?" He was appalled by the idea.

"No. Not to me. I know all your secrets. You told me
everything."

"I've never had that tendency before."

"You thought you were dreaming."

"You were here all along?" He was amazed.

"I slept with you."

He was appalled. "You risked yourself?"

She shrugged, as if at fate. "I love you. I need you. I want to marry you and have your children."

"Roberta, honey, you're just emotionally involved because you saved my life. Now you feel responsible for me. I know the Chinese think that way, but you're hardly Chinese. You don't have to marry me."

"Well, that's true. But if you love me, you need to take advantage of me and marry me now, while you have the opportunity."

"Today?" He felt his beard and frowned. He wasn't sure he had the strength even to shave.

"As soon as you're well enough."

He nodded thoughtfully. If this was one of his dreams, it was more coherent and better than any of the others. He closed his eyes and slept again.

When Ralph came and helped him to the bathroom, the operation had a familiarity of repetition. "You've helped me before."

"Not you. Some raving maniac who wasn't at all nice about it."

"I'm sorry."

"Roberta was here. She calmed you down."

"Yes." So she had been there.

Ralph smiled. "I'm a rotten patient, too. I hate being sick. I understood you."

"Thank you."

"You must be getting healthier. You're almost civilized."

Graham smiled ruefully. "I owe you a couple."

"Pass it on." He went by the bread-cast-on-the-waters theory.

Roberta had changed his bed and piled his pillows. She watched Ralph help Graham back into bed, then told the maintenance man thank-you. She brought a tray in, filled with nibbles and little ceramic jars of liquids to tempt a fussy, recuperating appetite.

She sat and watched him, listening as he remembered. "I had nightmares. I woke up in one of my dreams, and there was a demon on my chest, all eyes and hair. It scared the hell out of me."

"And you scared Buttercup. Poor baby came in and told me all about the demon in this bed. I agreed."

"That was Buttercup? That nasty-looking thing is named Buttercup?"

"Buttercup has surgically lost his interest in the opposite sex. They keep him to lend out to people who think they have mice."

Graham gave a thoughtful, noncommittal nod.

She just dropped it in. "Like . . . Gus."

He took too deep a breath into his recovering lungs and coughed and coughed and coughed.

She waited patiently, a little almost-smile on her sweet lips and a very knowing look in her eyes.

He finally couldn't continue the cough any longer, and he still hadn't thought of any defense for buying that mouse and setting Roberta up that way, so he just said a vague "Gus."

"You'll be delighted to hear that Milly sent him back as a get-well gift, but said not to put him in your room until you are well. We don't want a sick mouse on our hands."

"No."

"I've known since the night you shooed him out into the kitchen."

"No!"

"Yes. I saw the pellets scattered in your doorway. I peeked in and saw the cage while you were getting the snow shovel from the car. I puzzled it out. You sly and sneaky man. Outrageous!''

"You were very brave."

"I really was. I was magnificent. But you ought to have told me. When we buried Gus, I knew. And I realized you'd had him for a while. When I hit him, you were stunned. I'd seen him move and you said it was rigor mortis. That was so clever. But you had acted strangely. I dug up Gus, and the box was empty. So I finally asked Milly about it. She was brilliant in evading my questions until I told her what all had happened. Then she laughed and laughed and laughed. That's when I went to her office and saw the same kind of cage, and I remembered hearing Gus sing. Milly said that if I didn't make up my feeble mind about you pretty soon, she was going to steal you from me. She thinks you're special. So do I, Graham, so do I.''

"Then you're not just marrying me to have environmentalists?''

"I'm marrying you selfishly because I love you."

"My God. Do you know I tried for weeks to get sick so that you would notice me?''

"You told me that, too."

"Good grief."

"You either have to live pure, or you have to stay well. You tell everything. Do you remember Teri?''

He gasped.

"Uh-hmm. Even Teri."

"Well, that was just juvenile juices. That wasn't serious. But we might mention Jim and Robin right here." He was a little cranky. "They are serious men. Am I going to have to spend all my life shoving other men away from you?''

"No."

"Well, I won't tolerate—"

"You well know that no other man has ever interested me seriously."

He looked at her, and all the sham fell away. He finally knew she really loved him. He accepted it as
reality, not as a dream. She loved him. He smiled at
her. "Roberta, what did I ever do to actually capture
your attention?"

"Well, you walked into my apartment, and the only
thing that I could give myself as an excuse for allowing you around was that I'd never been susceptible to
blonds. You took my breath away. I wanted you right
then. Didn't you notice how I bent my time and en-
ergy and interests to you? I watched *football*! That
bloody, destructive game. And I loved it. All because
of you. I wanted you from the beginning, but when I
realized you'd left me to save a woman-baiting mouse,
I loved you. I will do what I must to make our lives
meet. That by itself should tell you how serious I am
about you."

"Me, too." He just wasn't as eloquent as she. But he
meant all those words, too.

And she understood.

He wanted her. He needed her then—in a realiza-
tion, a reestablishing of their commitment. She was so
tender with him, and she did understand, but she
wouldn't allow him to take control; he wasn't strong
enough. She took off her clothes as he watched, and
she did all the work, giving him quick, sweet release. It
was his contentment that pleasured her.

With him lax and sleepy, she could run her hands
along him and reassure herself that he was there with
her. That he had again survived. His illness had scared
her so badly, to see him so sick, and to feel so helpless.

She'd bullied everyone to get help for him. She'd not been very receptive to any hesitation. She'd been a little firm, almost rude.

Graham recovered fully. He was understanding about his car's newly pleated door and creased fender. And he was admitted into her sanctuary. Its fragrance was as hers, and her bed was a scented cloud, but she was all his reality.

They went to Texas a month after that and were married on April fifteenth. Everyone there complained about the Lamberts running so many weddings into one year and making the whole entire area tired of parties. Living that high off the hog, that many times a year, was just too much. Another party! They glared at Fredricka, saying she'd better wait for a while before she got hitched up.

She replied, "I'm going to be an old maid. I'm not getting married. Men are stupid."

Most of the women laughed and asked who was annoying her to that extent. They all knew it was Sling. He just didn't seem to realize he loved Fredricka. He treated her like a friendly cousin.

And they accosted Mr. Lambert, asking him to explain how come he had four daughters married to Yankees? Then they all sat back and waited for his reply.

He said, "You all well know we're supposed to save our Confederate money. Your daddies all told you that. With this infiltration, we're going to convert the whole kaboodle and the South will rise again! It was coming, but I thought the girls might just help it along."

When the newlyweds were ready to leave on their honeymoon, no one would let Graham go. "Run along, honey," they said to Roberta. "He'll catch up with you later. He's going to play the piano for us." That was what Pig said. He played oboe. Other instruments turned up magically, and it was an evening to remember. Sheet music was passed around, instruments were tuned, and the music began. It was lovely.

In the doorway to the solarium Roberta stood with her mother's arm around her and they smiled at each other. Like all the others, they listened. It was marvelous.

The newlyweds did get away, at last, and drove down to Padre Island. There, in a third-floor condo that overlooked the Gulf, the two lay replete on their bed, and they talked.

"You are a treasure," she told her husband. "All those people are awed by you."

"They just needed a piano player. After they found out at George's wedding that I could play, they probably threatened you with mayhem unless you snared me so they could all play together."

"Pig did mention they needed a piano player."

"You're a witch." He made that a thoughtful observation.

"You're a warlock. I had no intention of ever marrying, like Fred. I was going to devote my life to the environment."

"You still can." He thought about the words, then added, "A lot of your time. But you have to save some for me."

"I love you, Graham. I love you with all my heart."

"It's a good thing." He smiled at her and said, "Now *this* time, I want you to be calm and steady. Allow me to make some experiments and studies of the female body, and don't get so excited. Okay?"

"We'll see."

"It's just a matter of control. You're in charge. You can handle it. Be relaxed and just take it easy. Understand? It's good training. You are the master of your ship and the captain of your body. You can give me a little time to fool around. Right?"

"Quit talking so much."

He sighed. "You're already interested and eager. I knew it. We'll never have a leisurely session. It's all greed and hurry. No relaxed tasting."

She slid a hand down him. "Relaxed?"

"Don't get fresh."

She slid the hand up to his hairy hard chest, over his dear, scratchy face, down over his furry stomach and a little bit lower. He sucked in his breath and went rigid. She said, "Disinterested? Casual?"

"Well, maybe in a couple of decades."

She laughed, and hugged him. And they made sweet and tender love, relishing being alive, together, and in *this* world.

*   *   *   *   *

Silhouette Intimate Moments

NOW APPEARING!

LIEUTENANT GABRIEL RODRIGUEZ
in
Something of Heaven

From his first appearance in Marilyn Pappano's popular *Guilt by Association*, Lieutenant Gabriel Rodriguez captured readers' hearts. Your letters poured in, asking to see this dynamic man reappear—this time as the hero of his own book. This month, all your wishes come true in *Something of Heaven* (IM #294), Marilyn Pappano's latest romantic tour de force.

Gabriel longs to win back the love of Rachel Martinez, who once filled his arms and brought beauty to his lonely nights. Then he drove her away, unable to face the power of his feelings and the cruelty of fate. That same fate has given him a second chance with Rachel, but to take advantage of it, he will have to trust her with his darkest secret: somewhere in the world, Gabriel may have a son. Long before he knew Rachel, there was another woman, a woman who repaid his love with lies—and ran away to bear their child alone. Rachel is the only one who can find that child for him, but if he asks her, will he lose her love forever or, together, will they find *Something of Heaven*?

This month only, read *Something of Heaven* and follow Gabriel on the road to happiness.

Silhouette Intimate Moments®

NORA ROBERTS
brings you the first
Award of Excellence title
Gabriel's Angel
coming in August from
Silhouette Intimate Moments

They were on a collision course with love....

*Laura Malone was alone, scared—and pregnant. She was running
for the sake of her child. Gabriel Bradley had his own problems.
He had neither the need nor the inclination to get involved in
someone else's.*

*But Laura was like no other woman . . . and she needed him. Soon
Gabe was willing to risk all for the heaven of her arms.*

The Award of Excellence is given to one specially selected title per
month. Look for the second Award of Excellence title, coming out in
September from Silhouette Romance—**SUTTON'S WAY**
by **Diana Palmer**

Im 300-1

Coming in July from

Silhouette Desire®

ODD MAN OUT #505
by Lass Small

Roberta Lambert is too busy with her job to notice that her new apartment-mate is a strong, desirable man. But Graham Rawlins has ways of getting her undivided attention....

Roberta is one of five fascinating Lambert sisters. She is as enticing as each one of her three sisters, whose stories you have already enjoyed or will want to read:

- Hillary in GOLDILOCKS AND THE BEHR (Desire #437)

- Tate in HIDE AND SEEK (Desire #453)

- Georgina in RED ROVER (Desire #491)

Watch for Book IV of Lass Small's terrific miniseries and read Fredricka's story in TAGGED (Desire #528) coming in October.